He crouched, bringing himself eye to eye with her. "I thought you were going to bed."

"I wanted to finish this first."

He turned the pad around. "Is that how you see me?"

"Do you find fault with it?" Oh, he was so close. Close enough to steal a kiss before he could back away, if she dared.

"You make me look younger than I feel."

"A little bit of gray at the temples doesn't age you." She brushed at the gray with her fingers, then let them drift over his ears and down his jaw.

He drew a quick breath. "We can't do this," he said roughly, capturing her hand, holding it.

"Do what?"

"Any of this. It's too complicated. We barely know each other."

He was right, of course. What had gotten into her? It would be crazy—

"When we have the test results and know what we're dealing with, then we can make conscious, thought-out decisions," he added.

"You talk too much, cowboy lawyer."

He laughed softly and stood. It was obvious he wanted her. She hadn't overestimated him, not in the sketch and not in her mind.

She didn't want him to reject her, nor did she want to confuse their situation, so she got up from the chair and left, not looking back once, knowing he watched her, excited by the idea.

And hopefully leaving him wanting more.

RED VALLEY RANCHERS: Brothers who worked the land...side by side with the women they loved!

Dear Reader,

A Family, At Last is the second book in my Red Valley Ranchers series, and features another Ryder brother, Vaughn, who is about as opposite of my heroine as anyone can be. Does that stop them from falling in love, or do their differences enhance the relationship?

Since this is a romance novel, the answer is clear, but how they get there, how they learn to embrace each other's differences, is the fun part. Plus, at the heart of the story is six-year-old Cassidy, who was doing fine with just her father but who blooms when Karyn Lambert comes into her life.

I love these kinds of transformations, whether adult or child. I hope you do, too.

Susan

A Family, At Last

Susan Crosby

H HARLEQUIN® SPECIAL EDITION®

Recycling programs
for this product may
not exist in your area.

ISBN-13: 978-0-373-65772-8

A FAMILY, AT LAST

Copyright © 2013 by Susan Bova Crosby

Printed in U.S.A.

Books by Susan Crosby

Harlequin Special Edition

*The Bachelor's Stand-In Wife #1912
★The Rancher's Surprise Marriage #1922
*The Single Dad's Virgin Wife #1930
*The Millionaire's Christmas Wife #1936
ΔThe Pregnant Bride Wore White #1995
ΔLove and the Single Dad #2019
§The Doctor's Pregnant Bride? #2030
ΔΔAt Long Last, a Bride #2043
¤Mendoza's Return #2102
*Husband for Hire #2118
*His Temporary Live-In Wife #2138
*Almost a Christmas Bride #2157
§§Fortune's Hero #2181
ΩA Date with Fortune #2239
¶The Cowboy's Return #2266
¶A Family, At Last #2290

Silhouette Desire

**Christmas Bonus,
  Strings Attached #1554
**Private Indiscretions #1570
**Hot Contact #1590

**Rules of Attraction #1647
**Heart of the Raven #1653
**Secrets of Paternity #1659
  The Forbidden Twin #1717
  Forced to the Altar #1733
  Bound by the Baby #1797

*Wives for Hire
ΔThe McCoys of Chance City
**Behind Closed Doors
★Back in Business
§The Baby Chase
¤The Fortunes of Texas:
  Lost...and Found
§§The Fortunes of Texas:
  Whirlwind Romance
ΩThe Fortunes of Texas:
  Southern Invasion
¶Red Valley Ranchers

Other titles by this author
available in ebook format.

SUSAN CROSBY

believes in the value of setting goals, but also in the magic of making wishes, which often do come true—as long as she works hard enough. Along life's journey she's done a lot of the usual things—married, had children, attended college a little later than the average coed and earned a B.A. in English. Then she dove off the deep end into a full-time writing career, a wish come true.

Susan enjoys writing about people who take a chance on love, sometimes against all odds. She loves warm, strong heroes and good-hearted, self-reliant heroines, and she will always believe in happily-ever-after.

More can be learned about her at www.susancrosby.com.

With gratitude to Mary & Jim Rickert and Mark Estes of Prather Ranch, who believe in running a humane operation, because it's good for the animals, the land and the people, and who were so generous with their time and expertise.

And to my Lunch Bunch—
Lori, Nancy, Sheryl and Virginia. We've shared it all!

Chapter One

Karyn Lambert took yet another look at her rearview mirror. No doubt about it. She was being followed. Maneuvering her Beetle through heavy 6:00 p.m. traffic on Santa Monica Boulevard, she changed lanes—and so did the black SUV that had been tailing her since she'd left Disneyland an hour ago. And now, as she was pulling up at Sprinkles Cupcakes to pick up a well-earned red velvet treat, she had to make a decision. Go to the bakery's cupcake dispenser as planned and see if the guy in the SUV followed—or lose him in traffic?

Karyn inched past the bakery. All the street parking was taken. She weighed the risk of the parking garage nearby and rejected it after another quick glance at her mirror. Headlights and Christmas lights created a dark, distinctive silhouette of the driver.

"Man Wearing Cowboy Hat, you are following the wrong girl."

This was Karyn's turf. She knew how to zip through the side streets of Beverly Hills efficiently. It didn't take her long to leave the SUV in the dust and make a quick retreat to her Hollywood duplex, its garage tucked in the rear. She'd never been so grateful for that privacy before.

Grabbing her packages, she rushed upstairs to her unit, let herself in and slammed the door shut. She left the lights off, set down her bags on the kitchen table, then waited in the dark for fifteen minutes, going from window to window, peering through the blinds. Finally she turned on the living room light and sat on the sofa, her legs bouncing. *Why would someone follow her?* In the land of Hollywood-star wannabes, she was the least likely person to stalk.

Then again, maybe it was her imagination, a fanciful notion of her overtired brain. It was six days before Christmas, hell week in her line of work. She was exhausted, so maybe her mind was playing tricks on her.

Of course. That had to be it.

Shrugging it off, Karyn headed for the kitchen. The doorbell rang.

She froze.

When it rang again she stealthily made her way to the front door and looked through the peephole. She hadn't turned on her porch light, but she could make out the silhouette. A man in a cowboy hat.

"Ms. Lambert?" he asked through the door. "I know you're there. I just want a few words with you."

Not a snowflake's chance in—

"Please. I'm a lawyer. I'm looking for your brother, Kyle."

Stunned, she covered her mouth with her hand and took an involuntary step back.

"Turn your outside light on and look through the peephole. I'll show you my identification."

"Why do you want Kyle?" she asked.

A beat passed. "He's not in trouble, Ms. Lambert, but I also don't want to shout personal information through your door. I don't need much of your time."

She flipped on the porch light. "Prove who you are."

His driver's license told a basic story. Name, Vaughn Ryder. Six-foot-one, 180 pounds. Lean and rangy, she thought. Brown hair, blue eyes. Thirty-eight years old. Organ donor.

"What else have you got?"

He held up a business card. Under his name was a list: ranch and farm contracts, conservation easements, estate planning, water and power rights. His address said Ryder Ranch, Red Valley, California, with a P.O. box, phone numbers and an email address. She couldn't begin to imagine what a cowboy lawyer would want of Kyle, but she was curious enough to invite him in.

Karyn opened the door then stared for a few seconds. He was a cowboy all right, from his black hat down to his fancy stitched boots. A pristine white dress shirt with silver snaps was set off with a gorgeous bolo tie of silver and black. His black jeans were snug—

Definitely a man. And truly a cowboy, apparently, who matched his business card.

"Want to pat me down?" he asked, humor in his voice.

She struggled to look him in the eye. "What?"

"For weapons? I'd like to speak to you privately, and if you need to check me for weapons before you'll invite me in, I'm okay with that." He held his arms out, his briefcase dangling from one hand.

She took a couple of steps back and gestured him indoors, feeling heat in her face at being caught eyeing him. "You've been following me since I left Disneyland," she stated, noting his graying temples and the intensity of his blue eyes as he swept off his hat.

"Guilty. Actually, I've been behind you since you first left here this morning."

"Why?"

"I wanted to get a sense of your life. You shop a lot."

She laughed at the wonder in his voice, and it felt good, breaking the tension. "It's what I do for a living. I'm a personal shopper."

"That pays enough to make a living?"

"Are you implying that I make money some other way?" Ice coated her words. "I assure you everything I do is aboveboard."

"My apologies," he said with sincerity. "I didn't mean to imply that. Ignorance, that's all. May we sit?"

She sat, forgiving him for not understanding her

business, which encompassed much more than shopping. Her task list was even longer than those written on his business card.

"Why do you need a sense of *my* life?" she asked. "You said you're here about my twin brother."

"What I have to say involves you, but primarily Kyle, and he's the one I'd like to speak to first. I've been hunting for him but haven't come up with an address."

"You can't...." Karyn's throat burned as memories assaulted her. Hot, painful tears pressed at her eyes with such suddenness and force she barely managed to get words out. "You can't find him because he died, Mr. Ryder. He was killed in combat three years ago in Afghanistan."

She sat there for a moment, trying to tamp down the emotions that were still raw and unfiltered, even after all this time, but especially hard at Christmas. When she couldn't pull herself together, she hurried to her bedroom, shutting the door, leaning against it before falling on the bed, not caring that a stranger sat in her living room.

Vaughn stood automatically, then sank slowly into the chair when he realized she wasn't coming right back. *Kyle Lambert is dead.* Relief swept through him first. His life had just gotten much easier. Then he recalled the fresh grief in Karyn's eyes. He couldn't imagine losing any of his five siblings. The pain would be overwhelming.

Of course, none of it mattered at all if Kyle turned

out not to be the man Vaughn was seeking—or even the right Kyle Lambert. But seeing Karyn's curly light brown hair was its own kind of validation.

Unable to sit still, Vaughn wandered the room. A table was stacked neatly with wrapped Christmas presents, a color-coded tag on each one, but otherwise her apartment wasn't decorated for the holiday. On the wall were numerous paintings, mostly landscapes and floral themes. When he looked closer, he noticed Karyn Lambert's signature in the corner.

There were no photographs of any kind, not of people or places or events, which he found odd. Most women displayed pictures.

After a while a door clicked open. Karyn came into the living room, her eyes still damp. She was an attractive woman, not Hollywood-slim but nicely curved, more girl next door. Her height was a mystery because she was wearing very high heels. He'd noted her sexy walk all day as he'd followed her.

"I'm sorry," she said.

"I knew he was a marine, but I didn't know he'd passed away. I should've waited for my private investigator to dig deeper when I was given Kyle's name. He was out of the state on a job, and I was in a hurry to get results. I—I'm sincerely sorry for how I handled this."

"Dig deeper for what, Mr. Ryder?" she asked.

"Vaughn, please. Ms. Lambert, I believe your brother may have fathered a child with Ginger Donohue six years ago."

She dropped onto the sofa, her eyes wide. "Kyle has a child? A piece of him is still here?"

"It's a possibility. Since we can't do paternity testing with your brother, we can do relationship testing with you."

"I'm an aunt? Please tell me about— What's the child's name?"

"Cassidy." He pulled out his cell phone and brought up a photo.

"Oh." Karyn ran her fingers over the screen, tears pooling in her eyes again. "She's so beautiful."

"Yes."

"She kinda looks like Kyle."

And you, he thought. "Does the name Ginger Donohue ring a bell, Ms. Lambert?"

She shook her head. "I don't understand. Cassidy is six? Why would this woman wait so long to come forward?"

"Are you sure your brother didn't know?" Vaughn asked.

"I'm positive. He would've been there for his daughter, no doubt about it."

"I don't know why Ginger didn't tell Kyle, since obviously he was alive for the first three years of Cassidy's life."

"So, something changed. Is it money? I was the beneficiary of Kyle's death benefits, and I haven't spent much of it. It should go to his daughter—"

Vaughn stopped her with a gesture. "Ginger walked out of Cassidy's life two years ago."

Karyn leaned back abruptly, staring at him but her gaze not really connecting, then a slow dawning of excitement came over her.

"When do I get to pick her up?" She looked around her space. "I'll need a bigger place. Near a park. I'll have to check out schools." She smiled and looked directly at Vaughn. "Where is she now? When do I get her?"

He ignored her bubble of happiness. He had to. "If the testing confirms she's Kyle's daughter, you'll meet her, of course, and be part of her life. But, Ms. Lambert, she won't be living with you. I've been her father since the day she was born. I'm not giving her up."

Chapter Two

"You've been her...father?" Karyn shook her head, confused. "I don't— Did you know she wasn't yours?"

He nodded. "Ginger was pregnant when we met, but we didn't get married until Cassidy was a month old. The birth certificate lists the father as unknown." Vaughn walked to her front window and looked out. "I asked for years to adopt Cass, but Ginger put me off. Then she left. That's why I started the search for the biological father. I want to legally make her mine."

Karyn's mind spun as shock piled atop shock. She hardly knew what to think, except that this woman, Ginger, must be the epitome of femininity to attract both Kyle, a regular guy, and this Vaughn, who was a cut above. Apparently neither man had seen her for her true self.

"We ran into a lot of dead ends because so many years had elapsed," Vaughn said, his back still turned to Karyn. "An old roommate of Ginger's provided the name Kyle Lambert as a possibility. After that it was a matter of connecting the dots, but I'm still not sure it's your brother. We had a name. There are others of the same name and age around the country. Do you know if he lived in San Francisco seven years ago?"

"No, but that doesn't mean he didn't visit."

Vaughn came back and sat down, resting his arms on his thighs and focusing on Karyn again. "I'm sorry for the pain this is causing you, reliving your brother's death."

"It's never far from my mind, but now there's joy, too, if Cassidy is his child." She touched his arm. "I can see this is hard for you, too."

"Harder for Cassidy. She was old enough to feel the abandonment but without any context to understand it. She used to ask about her mother, but it's rare now. I have no good explanation to give her anyway. We just carry on. Fortunately, I have a big, generous family. She's well loved."

Karyn believed him. But now that the shock was abating, a hunger to know Kyle's child took precedence. "I haven't had dinner yet," she said. "Would you like to join me?" She needed to do something normal—heat up a can of soup or leftover pizza, which was all she had on hand. They could talk more while they ate.

"I have a flight to catch. I'm already cutting it close." He opened his briefcase then passed her a tube containing a swab. "You just scrape the inside of your cheeks," he said, gesturing.

She eyed the item. "What about chain of custody?"

His brows went up. "Pardon?"

"One of my clients is a regular on *Crime and Punishment,* so I watch it every week."

He smiled, which had been her goal. "You're an expert then."

"Absolutely. I know the way this is supposed to be done. The specimen should be collected by a neutral third party, like at a lab."

"I can arrange for that, although this would be a civil case, not criminal, so the same rules don't apply." He sat back, more relaxed than he'd been earlier. "I'll make a deal with you. If it comes back negative for Kyle as the father, we can redo it through every legal step."

She thought that over. "I guess you're just looking for the truth—not playing any games."

"If you knew me better, that wouldn't be a question. Plus, I'm an officer of the court. As an expert in, uh, television justice, you understand what that means."

She smiled at his attempt to bring humor to the situation. "Yeah. Okay."

Karyn felt awkward doing the test in front of him, not looking at him as she did so, then dropping the swab into the tube and passing it to him. He tucked it into a padded envelope then into his briefcase, their own chain of custody.

He stood, so she did, too. "No matter how this turns out, I enjoyed meeting you," he said and headed to the door. "May I ask where you were going before you so effectively ditched me? Nice job of that, by the way."

She smiled. "The ATM at Sprinkles for a red velvet cupcake."

"They sell cupcakes from an ATM?"

"Well, that's what they call it. It dispenses one at a time." She shrugged. "I'd had a long day."

His hand was on the doorknob. "You went to the happiest place on Earth."

"I shopped there. Don't get me wrong, I love Disneyland, but when you go inside to purchase gifts for clients and don't even get to take one ride on Space Mountain, it's not a fun trip."

"I've never been to Disneyland."

"Are you serious? You've never taken Cassidy? We have to correct that."

The air between them felt heavy with sudden tension.

"Maybe we will," he said finally. "Good night, Karyn. Try not to get too anxious waiting."

"Fat chance."

"I know." He left.

Karyn wandered back into the living room to look out the window. She saw him walk up the street and out of sight. He must've parked where she wouldn't be able to see him coming.

After a minute his car went past. He gave her a wave.

"You're a nice guy, Vaughn Ryder, cowboy lawyer," she said out loud. "But if you think you're going to make all the decisions and I'm going to go along with them without discussion, you're crazy." She'd already missed six years of her niece's life.

She knew she was counting on being that sweet little girl's aunt way too much to be healthy, but Karyn needed something to get her through Christmas, which was always a tough time of year for her.

Her stomach growled, reminding her she hadn't eaten since breakfast, but the soup and leftover pizza didn't appeal. In fact, nothing sounded good, so she went into her bedroom to get paper to wrap the presents she'd purchased today. She would drop them off in the morning to her clients, along with the ones stacked on her dining table.

She couldn't wait to get them out of her house. They were a painful reminder of how little she had to look forward to with her trip home to visit her parents on Christmas, no longer a day that they celebrated. For a month she'd shopped for everyone else, but she hadn't bought a single present herself to give. She didn't even go through the motions.

Sometimes it just about killed her.

She'd finished the seventh of ten packages when her doorbell rang. She looked through the peephole, wondering if Vaughn had come back. Kind of hoped he had, actually, but it was a stranger.

"Who is it?" she asked.

"Delivery from Mr. Ryder for Ms. Lambert."

Surprised and curious, she opened the door.

"Here you go," a teenage boy said then took the stairs three at a time, hopping out of sight.

Karyn knew what it was without looking at the logo on the box. The incredible scents of chocolate and vanilla, and a hint of lemon, filled her head as she carried the box to the kitchen and opened it, finding a dozen cupcakes, three of them red velvet.

She found herself grinning as she peeled the paper off one and took a big bite, closing her eyes and savoring the treat, eating the whole thing before she picked up his business card and dialed the cell number listed.

"Vaughn Ryder," he said.

"I devoured one. I expect it's not the last I'll have tonight."

"I figure I owed you that much."

She heard the smile in his voice. "Thank you. It was very thoughtful. I hope you got one for yourself."

"Two. Red velvet and chocolate marshmallow."

She waited a beat. "Vaughn? Would you do something for me?"

"If I can."

Cagey. But then, he was a lawyer. "Would you give Cassidy an extra hug for me? For Kyle. She won't know, but…"

"I can do that."

Karyn heard the sound of a jet in the background and figured he'd arrived at LAX. "One more thing," she said before letting him go. "If Cassidy is Kyle's daughter, I'm going to want more than just to be a part of her life."

"What do you mean?"

"I'm not sure what my rights might be. You probably know better than I do, but I'll find out. There was something in his will about heirs. I'll have to look it up. Have a safe flight."

She tucked the phone under her chin. Yes, a nice guy.

But she still wouldn't cut him any slack when it came to Kyle's daughter.

It was after midnight when Vaughn got home. Cassidy was staying with his parents, so his four-bedroom, two-story house seemed especially quiet. Each of Jim and Dori Ryder's children had been gifted a piece of land on Ryder Ranch property on their twenty-first birthday, and Vaughn had chosen his without ever expecting to build on it. In fact, he'd never thought he'd live on the ranch after he'd left for college, anticipating law school then fulfilling a dream of life and work in San Francisco, his favorite city.

Funny how having a child could change so much.

Vaughn climbed the staircase, went into Cassidy's room and switched on the light. The walls were painted her favorite denim blue. Rows of running horses were printed across her bedspread. She'd named every one of them. The only doll in sight was dressed as a cowgirl, a lasso in her hand and tiny red hat on her head.

A wall shelf holding framed photographs drew Vaughn. There was one of the two of them when she was a few minutes old, another when she'd sat her first horse alone at age two. A group photo of the entire family was tucked behind the others and was the only photo of her mother on display. The picture had been taken at a Fourth of July barbecue. Everyone had worn red, white and blue.

Vaughn slipped it out. He hadn't put away Ginger's photos after she left, but Cassidy had. Vaughn would find them hidden in various drawers upon opening them. He'd left them alone. Finally she'd stacked them in a box and handed it to him.

"Please put her away," she'd said, looking much older than her age.

He had, but she'd kept the one, even though they'd taken other family photos more recently. She hadn't given up on her mother completely.

He'd kept Ginger's farewell note because it was proof she'd voluntarily given her to Vaughn. It hadn't said much. "I've had enough. Cassidy's yours. She's the one you want anyway."

She was right about that.

Too wound up to sleep, Vaughn went to his office. He booted his laptop and opened personal shopper Karyn Lambert's Facebook page. There were photos and testimonials from a few clients, including Josh Renard, the *Crime and Punishment* star she'd mentioned, and Gloriana Macbeth, a major Hollywood star.

Karyn's publicity photo showed a competent-looking but also sexy woman. Under different circumstances he might have accepted her dinner invitation. He bet she'd have some interesting stories to tell.

The long day caught up with him. He shut down the computer then went upstairs to his bedroom. He had nothing to unpack except the tube with the swab in it. He would package it well tomorrow and send it to a private lab in San Francisco.

And then the wait would start.

Chapter Three

"I'll pay you double," Gloriana Macbeth said, her voice oozing with the charm that had landed her many headliner movie roles.

Karyn rolled her eyes. She was at home talking on her Bluetooth, having just finished wrapping two last-minute purchases for her clients. She would deliver them, pack her suitcase and head for the airport for a red-eye flight to visit her parents in Vermont, a visit she dreaded more than anything.

Karyn drew a deep breath and focused on the phone call. "Tomorrow's Christmas Eve, Glori."

"Seriously? You're going to use the Christmas card, pun intended? How long have we worked together? I know you don't celebrate the holiday," Gloriana said dryly.

"I still spend the time with my parents."

"Ah, yes. Where you sit and watch TV and get through the days trying to avoid anything Christmas-like."

Bull's-eye. Direct hit. "Still…you've got a stylist."

"She went into labor this morning," Gloriana said. "And I'm between assistants, as you know. I do wish you would accept that job."

The woman went through personal assistants with staggering frequency. She was the perfect stereotype of a diva, nicknamed Lady Macbeth for her ruthless ambition. Karyn preferred their friendly-but-not-a-daily relationship.

"Come on, Karyn. I'll triple your fee. What'll it take? An hour, maybe? Just show up, help me choose a gown and accessories, then you're done. You know I don't trust just anyone, and this is for the cover of *People*."

If the woman would just once say please, Karyn might have said yes. "Glori—"

"Quadruple, but that's it. It should cover your airfare, then you could take another vacation somewhere else to recover from this one," Gloriana said. "I've already had hair and makeup done."

"All right, all right," Karyn said to get her off her back and because she needed the distraction. It had been excruciating, waiting for the DNA results.

"In an hour." She hung up without a thank you or goodbye.

"You're welcome," Karyn said into the air. Most of her clients were reasonable and polite, although they sometimes displayed a certain entitlement that often came with celebrity. She continued to keep Gloriana as a client for the status of having a megastar on her list, but also because they'd figured out how to work together with minimal fuss after a rocky beginning five years ago.

Karyn didn't claim to be a stylist, although she could have been. She didn't like to focus on only one kind of job, preferring variety instead. Except it had become harder and harder to get up every morning and do the work since Kyle had died.

Karyn grabbed her purse and the packages, pushing thoughts of Kyle from her head, wanting to arrive at the photo studio before Gloriana and look over the gown choices from her favorite designer, which would've been sent ahead of her arrival.

Traffic was a bear. What should have been a half-hour trip became almost an hour, giving Karyn no time to set up early. She didn't like being rushed in general, but today was worse than usual. The combination of being late, Christmas Eve only a day away, the anticipated flight and the elusive test results were almost too much to handle.

But because she was a professional who took pride in her work, she put a smile on her face and knocked on the studio door, which was locked to the general public.

"Is she here?" Karyn asked the studio assistant, Fleur.

"Not yet." Fleur smiled sympathetically. "Oops. Strike that. Here she comes."

Karyn slipped past Fleur and into the dressing room. Eight gowns hung on a rack. Shelves were filled with shoes and accessories.

Gloriana came in immediately after, wearing a jogging suit that probably cost what Karyn made in a month. It emphasized Gloriana's perfect body, made so by hard work—exercise and healthy eating—and a little help from her plastic surgeon. She looked far younger than her thirty-three years.

"There you are," Gloriana said to Karyn.

"Yes, here I am. Good morning," Karyn said, smiling serenely, feeling anything but calm.

"Mimosa, Ms. Macbeth?" Fleur asked, passing her a glass without waiting for a response. "I have a tray of pastries, also."

"That's not the way to keep one's girlish figure." She glanced at Karyn, as if to make a point. "So, what have you chosen?"

Karyn took one gown off the rack. It dazzled with sparkling beads. "This salmon would look wonderful with your skin." Knowing Gloriana never said yes to the first selection, Karyn held up a teal silk charmeuse, her first choice. "Or this."

Gloriana flipped through the rest of the gowns, their metal hangers zinging along the rack. "These won't work."

Karyn stared at her. "None of them?"

"I believe you have excellent hearing, Karyn."

"Maybe if you try on the teal—"

"Call Lorenzo. Have him send over more."

"It's two days before Christmas, Glori. That's not a request we can make. And you know if he had more that he thought would work, he would've sent more."

Gloriana spun toward Karyn. "Are you telling me *no?*"

"You said it would take an hour of my time. I have other clients to help today and a plane to catch." Karyn held up the two gowns she'd selected. "Either of these would be perfect for the cover. Choose."

Gloriana stalked to the closest mirror. "I can't do the shoot now. Look at my face. It's all blotchy!"

Karyn's stomach churned so violently she could hardly swallow. Stupid. She'd been so stupid. And yet it was all so silly to her, absolutely inane, to be rejecting perfectly beautiful gowns on a whim. So much was more important in the world.

But she'd never been rude to any of her clients, even when they'd provoked her enough to deserve rudeness in return. She prided herself on her self-control.

"I apologize," Karyn said. "But I still can't do what you ask."

"I'm going to cut you some slack," Glori said, coming up close, "since I know this is a hard time of year for you. You've been blunt, so I will be, too. I strongly recommend you take some time off and figure out if this is what you want to do because more and more I have observed that you've lost enthusiasm for it. Get back to painting, which you've been saying for years that you wanted to do."

Karyn couldn't do anything but nod. Her burning throat had closed tighter. She could barely breathe.

Gloriana cupped Karyn's arm, which just about undid her. No one touched her these days.

"You've stopped talking about friends," Glori said. "Or about going places and doing things, the way you did when you first came to work for me. I see in you what happened to me. You've stopped caring. Maybe you've stopped trusting, too. You feel abandoned by your brother, even though he didn't die by choice. I know what that's like. And, no, I'm not going to explain that. Just trust that I'm telling you the truth.

"Now, you can be like me and hide behind roles, or you can rediscover yourself and enjoy the life your brother would want you to have. But make up your mind, Karyn. Don't let grief swallow you up anymore."

Karyn nodded her head several times, was tempted to hug the woman yet wouldn't be the one to instigate it, but then Gloriana walked away, the moment gone.

Karyn wanted to find joy again, to live the life Kyle would want for her, that she wanted for herself, but she didn't know how to change it. She was hungry to share the news with someone, anyone, that he might have a daughter, and she wanted to meet her and hold her and love her, as he would've done if he'd known. She couldn't tell anyone yet. Not even her parents, who still couldn't talk about Kyle, even when Karyn tried to get them to open up about him and share their memories.

By rote, Karyn delivered her final purchases then

drove home and packed her suitcase. Finished, she sank to the bed, shaking.

"I can't do this," she said, her face in her hands. She'd rather be alone than live through another Christmas like the three previous ones with her parents.

She didn't hesitate another second but canceled her flight then called her mother—and lied.

"I've got a sinus infection, Mom. The doctor says I can't fly. Maybe I can reschedule in a couple of weeks."

"You do sound stuffy."

Because she'd spent an hour straight crying.

"Karyn," her mother said then stopped.

"What, Mom?"

There was a long pause, then she said softly, almost apologetically, "We have a tree this year."

Shock slammed into Karyn. What did that mean? Should she see if she could get her seat back on the plane?

No. She wouldn't be able to keep the news about Cassidy to herself. She couldn't give her parents that kind of hope, especially if they were finally coming out of their grief.

For the first time in years they wished each other a Merry Christmas.

Feeling hollow, she pressed Vaughn Ryder's number on her cell phone. After five rings she was about to hang up when she heard him say hello.

"It's Karyn Lambert," she said, trying to shake off her tenuous emotions.

"Karyn."

Not a good start, she thought. He was all cool and businesslike. "I was wondering about the test results."

She didn't hear him sigh, but she was sure he had. "As I told you in an email yesterday, I saw you on Thursday. On Friday I shipped the sample. The lab was closed Saturday and Sunday, so they didn't receive it until today. And, yes, they did receive it. I checked. It takes seven to ten days for results."

"Oh."

"I understand that you're anxious, but we can't hurry the process."

"I just feel so far away."

"I would agree that 550 miles is a long way. It's almost to Oregon." After a brief pause, he said, "The Huntsman's Lodge is near our ranch. If you'd like to come up at some point and be nearby when the results are in, you're welcome to. But if your brother isn't the father, it'd be a useless trip."

"I'll think about it. Thanks."

"Merry Christmas, Karyn."

"And to you. And Cassidy."

Take some time off. Gloriana's words echoed in her head as Karyn hung up the phone. Now that she'd canceled her trip home, she could take Vaughn's suggestion and drive north. Hang out nearby.

She looked up the motel on her cell phone, then checked the time. If she left at four in the morning, she could be only thirty miles from Ryder Ranch between four and five in the afternoon. She'd researched everything last week, hopeful, saving the route on her phone's GPS.

Karyn reserved a room, then gathered up the gifts she'd already bought and wrapped for Cassidy, although not in Christmas wrap...just in case. Making several trips to her garage, she stowed everything so that she could just get up and go. She drove to a nearby gas station and filled her tank, then stopped at a market to pick up food for the journey. In the stationery products section of the grocery store she spotted a sketch pad. On impulse she tossed it in her cart.

That evening Karyn didn't think she would sleep but she drifted right off, which meant she'd made the right decisions, she thought when she awakened hours later, clear-headed, at 3:45 a.m. Traffic was heavy, even then, at least until she got about an hour out of town. Then it was just a long drive with only music and her thoughts to keep her company.

She stopped every couple of hours and stretched, had something to eat, then got going again. She hit traffic again in Sacramento. After that it was smooth sailing until, almost thirteen hours after she'd started, she pulled into the motel parking lot, feeling like she'd played a game of tackle football.

It would be dark soon. She would find a place to get a warm meal then go to her room and crash.

But as she walked toward the office, she slowed, then stopped. Her brother's daughter could be thirty miles away....

Karyn got back into her car, grabbed her directions and started driving. She didn't know what she would tell Vaughn when she got there. She didn't even know if she could find his house within the ranch property, but she'd spotted what looked like might be his on Google Earth. She assumed the small, private roads visible from high in the sky would be marked in some way. Except if she didn't get there before dark, she would probably have to abandon her quest.

For today.

Luck was on her side. The ranch itself was marked with a large sign. She followed her Google photo of the property, took a side road, then another, then another. Just when she thought she was lost, a house appeared, two stories and beautiful, surrounded by trees and with a paddock and barn behind it. A hitching rail stood in front of the house, which made her smile.

"Well, Karyn, you're not in Hollywood anymore," she said, staring.

As she sat in her car admiring the house and land, awareness of her actions the past twenty-four hours washed over and through her. She'd reacted emotionally to Gloriana Macbeth's normal behavior—she'd overreacted, that is. She hadn't thought through the potential consequences of showing up here. There was a child involved who had already been hurt by her mother's abandonment. Karyn couldn't contribute to that pain.

She restarted her engine. She would return to the motel, as planned. She would be patient and wait for the test results. So what if she was alone for Christmas?

As Karyn put the car in gear, the front door opened and the cowboy lawyer came out.

He didn't look happy.

Chapter Four

Annoyance wrapped around Vaughn like a lasso on a bucking bronc, pulling tighter and tighter as he went down his steps and headed to the electric blue VW Bug parked in front of his house.

She climbed out. Even angry, he acknowledged he was as impressed with her now as he was the first time he met her. Her super-tall heeled boots gave her height, and her fashionable clothes showed off a body he'd recalled with clarity several times in the past few days, but she also looked totally out of place for the environment.

And...fragile.

Which didn't stop him from laying into her. "What the hell are you doing here?"

"Leaving," she said, looking panicked. "I'm sorry. Honestly, I wasn't thinking. I'll go right now." She eyed the house. "Did Cassidy see me?"

"She's baking cookies with my mother at my parents' house."

Some of the tension left Karyn's face. "Thank goodness."

"Why are you here?"

She closed her eyes briefly, as if in pain. "You invited me."

"I believe I told you there was a motel nearby where you could wait for the test results, which won't be in for at least a week."

"I needed to get out of town."

"You made the FBI's Most Wanted list?"

She shook her head but said nothing.

"Why did you need to get out of town?" She hadn't seemed like a flighty woman, but appearances could be deceiving. He'd learned that the hard way.

"Christmas isn't a…good time of year for me. I usually fly to Vermont to see my parents, but I canceled the trip."

The fragility was there, still, in her face, especially her eyes. "Why isn't it a good time of year for you?" Then he remembered. He'd learned that her brother had died on Christmas Eve. It took some of the steam out of him, allowing a little sympathy to worm its way into his irritation.

"You ask hard questions," she said, sort of smiling. "A lot of factors went into my decision, including get-

ting angry at Gloriana Macbeth. I'm always well be-
haved in public, but this time I wasn't."

An image of the many-times proclaimed sexiest
woman alive flashed in Vaughn's head. "I read she was
a client of yours."

"She *was*."

"Ouch. That bad?"

Karyn shrugged. "It was suggested that I take some
time off."

He didn't want to know more, didn't want to see the
hurt in her eyes any longer. Didn't want any kind of
attachment to her. He'd always been drawn to women
who needed taking care of. He recognized it as his
fatal flaw.

"I just wanted to meet my niece," she said quietly.

"That hasn't been—"

"Confirmed. I know. I just feel it in my bones."

"I need hard fact."

She sighed. "I know." She looked around. "It's gotten dark. I need to go while I can still see the roads.
I'm sorry I bothered you."

She was too late. He heard his mother's truck head
up the driveway. As soon as the vehicle stopped, Cassidy jumped out and raced to Vaughn. She had red and
green frosting not only on her clothes but also in her
hair, the same sprung curls as Karyn's, although blond
rather than light brown.

Vaughn stumbled over the introductions, especially
when Karyn's eyes glistened. He gave her name but
nothing else. His mother, her short blond hair hidden

by her usual straw cowboy hat, looked at him curiously, but Cassidy just offered her hand to shake.

"Nice to meet you," his daughter said, like an adult, to Karyn.

"Same here." Karyn looked like she wanted to scoop up Cassidy and never let go.

Cassidy peeked into Karyn's car. "Do you live in there?" she asked, her green eyes going wide.

Karyn laughed. "No, but it's full, isn't it? I'm traveling."

"Are you staying with us?"

Karyn didn't take her eyes off Cassidy. "I have reservations at a motel nearby."

"But why are you here?"

"She came to paint, Cass. She's an artist." He ignored the way Karyn fired daggers at him with her eyes as he winged an answer he hoped his daughter would accept.

"Paint what?" Cass asked.

"Whatever interests me," Karyn said.

"Oh!" Cassidy's eyes went wide, then she jumped up and down. "It's my turn! It's my turn, isn't it? Finally. Right, Daddy? My official family portrait."

"Um…" Karyn took a couple of steps back, panic having replaced the daggers. "I don't—"

Cassidy hugged her father. "Oh, boy! Come on, Karyn. I'll show where it's going to go."

"Sweetheart," Vaughn said, putting his hands on her shoulders to still her. "Karyn needs to get back to the motel."

"But it's dark."

"Cars have headlights."

"Cass has a point," his mother said, a twinkle in her eyes.

Little escaped her. She'd obviously seen there'd been some misperceptions going on.

"She should stay here with us," Cass said, looking triumphant.

"What?" Vaughn and Karyn said at the same time.

"You have enough room," his mother said. "It'll be so much better than driving back and forth. That's a long trip to make every day."

"Oh, I couldn't," Karyn said, but everyone looked at Vaughn.

"Sure you can," Cassidy said. "The Ryders are always good hosts, right, Grammie? Right, Daddy? We are known for it," she added because she'd heard it said for her entire life.

Vaughn felt stuck at first, then he realized he'd been given a great opportunity. She could observe him and his daughter for a couple of days and see what a team they were, how much love they shared, what a good parent he was. The setup could be the advantage he needed to convince her not to take him to court over custody—or whatever plan she had in mind. She'd mentioned instructions in a will—

No, she couldn't win custody, even shared. *Probably.* But he didn't want to hedge his bets.

"Of course you should stay here," he said. "I'm sorry I didn't make that clear sooner."

"And you'll come to dinner at the homestead to-night," his mother added.

"Oh, no. Thank you but no. I can't intrude on family time."

Since when? Vaughn wondered. Maybe it had been her plan all along.

"Nonsense, dear. There's plenty of food. You might be overwhelmed by the sheer numbers of us—not only our family but our staff, too. It's a little chaotic but fun." She gave Cassidy a kiss. "We'll see you later, all cleaned up."

"Go hop in the shower," Vaughn told his daughter when his mother's truck was out of sight. "Shampoo twice."

"Okay, Daddy." She skipped off then hopped the stairs one at a time, her boots hitting each step hard. She slipped them off before she went into the house.

Karyn rounded on Vaughn. "What does she mean about a portrait?"

"All the kids have a portrait done at around this age. She's well aware of it and has been pressing me to have hers done."

"I don't do portraits." Once again panic had set in her eyes, joining her fear or anger or whatever else she was feeling.

"I saw your art in your apartment—"

She laughed, high and harsh. "The last time I was home my mother insisted I take them with me. I did them in high school. I took pictures and copied them. That's right. Be scared. I can't follow through with what you just promised. I might be able to sketch her if I practice a lot, but paint a portrait?"

"You have to."

She blew out a breath and stared at the ground. "I don't even have any equipment."

"We'll figure something out. Will you try?"

"Of course I'll try. Just lower your expectations, okay?" Karyn looked toward the house. "She's adorable. I'm sorry for the situation I put you in, but I'm glad I got to see her and glad I'll spend time with her."

"It's fine. Let's unload your car."

Karyn couldn't get a read on him. She figured he would be so angry with her, but he just seemed…contained.

He reached into her car and hauled out her bags. He picked up the largest suitcase and her garment bag and stood back while she got the others. His mouth quirked up on one side, making him seem years younger than thirty-eight. He was ten years older than she. His graying temples didn't age him as much as his weathered face, as if he'd been in the sun a lot—or had lived a hard life. She followed him to the house. "You told me before that you have a big family. Does that include siblings?"

"I have three brothers and two sisters. I'm the oldest. The youngest is in her last semester in college. She just got home last night for Christmas." He opened the door then let her precede him.

Inside, Karyn stopped and stared at the beautiful house. Home, she corrected herself, because it looked comfortable and was filled with personal items like

photographs and original art, not all of it Western.
Wood dominated but not overwhelmingly. The fur-
niture was slightly oversized, the upholstery inviting.
He had a fondness for tabletop-size sculptures, mostly
free-form but a few horses, too.

"You coming?" he asked from the top of the staircase.

A suitcase in each hand, she rushed up to meet him
then followed him down a hall.

"Did you expect to stay a month?" he asked, nod-
ding toward her suitcases.

"I didn't know what the weather would be." She
hefted one of them. "Shoes."

His brows lifted, and she challenged him with a stare
in return, daring him to comment.

"That's Cass's room on the right," he said, not pur-
suing the subject. "You're on the left."

"And where are you?"

"The other end on the same side as yours. Don't go
getting any ideas, though. I lock my door at night."

"I didn't—I mean, I won't—"

He laughed. "Just kidding."

She sort of laughed, too, if a little shakily.

"My door's always unlocked." He disappeared into
what would be her room, still chuckling to himself.

She liked that he'd teased her, even if it had caught
her off guard. Their time together would go much
smoother if they could relax enough to joke around
with each other.

"This is beautiful, Vaughn, as is the rest of your home."

"Thanks." He eyed her. "Is there anything left to bring upstairs?"

"Nothing I need at the moment." She would leave Cassidy's gifts in the car for now. They weren't Christmas gifts, after all. "What's the dress code for tonight?"

"We're casual on Christmas Day, but we'll dress up a little tonight. Not like a fancy dress or anything, but your best jeans and a sweater or something."

Karyn realized she'd been smiling for a while now. Her best jeans? That was easy. "What time?"

"We'll head over as soon as Cass is ready. Will that give you enough time?"

"Works for me."

"I'll leave you to it then." He went out the door, pulling it shut behind him.

Karyn opened her garment bag and hung up her clothes, finding the outfit she was looking for and leaving the remainder of the unpacking for later. The guest room seemed huge without him. Like the rest of his house, there were no frills here, but it wasn't sterile either. Plus it had a private bath.

Her reflection confirmed how tired she was, but a good night's sleep would cure that. For tonight, his family would be a distraction at a time she needed it most.

Karyn changed into a dark green V-neck sweater with sparkles through it, black skinny jeans and a pair of spiky black heels dotted with rhinestones. She added sparkly snowflake earrings and necklace, spritzed on a little vanilla perfume, then dabbed on some lip gloss.

Her goal tonight was not to get caught staring at Cassidy. Vaughn would understand her obsession, but the rest of his family might think differently.

Karyn could hear Vaughn talking to Cassidy in her room, so she went downstairs to wait. She'd just taken a seat in the living room when Vaughn and Cassidy joined her. Cassidy's hair was still damp, her curls distinct. She wore jeans shoved into boots that were dressier than the ones she'd left on the porch and a pale blue sweater with snowflakes knitted into it.

"You look very festive," Karyn said to her. "Christmassy," she explained when the little girl frowned.

"So do you. I like your sweater." She raced toward the front door. The girl always seemed to be running.

Karyn saw Vaughn's gaze drop to her chest. "I like your sweater, too. And your shoes, Hollywood."

Karyn laughed at the nickname. She slipped her jacket on as they went outdoors into the chilly night. "Do you get snow here?"

"Yes," Vaughn answered. "Although more on Gold Ridge Mountain than on the ground here. We get enough snow days to make the schoolkids happy."

"It keeps Bigfoot away," Cassidy said. She hopped into the backseat of the truck.

"Bigfoot lives here?"

"Oh, yes," Cassidy said. "And we have lots of UFOs, too. That's unidentified flying objects."

"My goodness." Karyn fastened her seatbelt. "Have you seen one?"

"Not yet. When I'm older I'm going to camp out on the mountain and see for myself. I'm skeptical."

Karyn laughed at that, noting Vaughn smiled as he put the truck in gear and took off. "I imagine you're on winter break from school."

"For two whole weeks. I'm in first grade. We have so much homework to do. I ride the bus."

"I rode the bus to school, too," Karyn said. "From kindergarten to eleventh grade."

"Why did you stop?"

"My brother bought a car. He drove." The happy memory was welcome, something she hadn't thought about for a while.

"I wish I had a brother to drive me," Cassidy said. "I don't like riding the bus. It takes *forever*. Hours."

"Twenty minutes," Vaughn said, glancing at his rear-view mirror.

Cassidy giggled. Apparently it was an ongoing complaint and correction between them.

"The homestead," Vaughn said, pulling between two other pickup trucks, with several others parked around the property.

"Are we late?"

"Nope. We're flexible. Everyone has jobs to do, regardless of the holiday, then they need time to get dressed up for the occasion. Whatever works."

"The house is huge," Karyn said after she got out.

"Eight bedrooms. They remodeled not too long ago,

opened the kitchen and dining room to the living room. They're anxious for enough grandchildren to fill the bedrooms." Cassidy jumped into his arms, and he carried her across the yard of the sprawling two-story structure, while Karyn navigated the dirt terrain. A lit Christmas tree was framed by a huge window. Colored lights hung along the eaves and windows, twinkling in the night sky, like the Christmases of her childhood, prompting a twinge of nostalgia for those wonderful times. She couldn't even blame her parents for their lack of interest now either because she didn't even decorate her own apartment.

Inside it was magical, with reflections of Christmas everywhere. A roaring fire burned in the hearth below an enormous mantel, where eleven stockings hung. Music competed with laughter. Karyn's head spun from the cacophony of sights and sounds. Everything was bigger than her own memories of the occasion, more magnificent.

"Here you are," Vaughn's mother said, making her way through the crowd.

"Hi, Grammie!"

"Hello, sweet girl. No more red and green hair."

"I ate it off. Well, some of it," she said with a glance at her father. "It was good!"

He ruffled her hair.

"C'mere, Karyn. I want to show you the portraits," Cassidy said.

Karyn followed her into a hallway that held many doors. There was a painting next to each door.

"See?"

Karyn almost choked. Each portrait was of a child sitting atop a horse. A horse! It was bad enough she was supposed to paint a human being, but a horse?

"This is my Daddy's room." She pointed to a boy on a horse, wearing all the requisite cowboy riding gear. He looked to be about Cassidy's age, as did the rest of the children as they continued down the hall. "I want to wear sparkly shoes. Like yours."

Then Cassidy took off to join a few other children, older and younger. Karyn followed more slowly, in a daze. Vaughn met her at the door into the living room.

"You could've told me," she said. "I can't do that. A horse? An entire body? I might've fudged a normal, chest-up portrait, but not that. No way. No how."

"We'll figure out something."

His mother came up to them. "Is everything okay?"

"Um, yes, thank you. I've seen some incredible homes," Karyn said, gathering composure. "But nothing that compares to this, Dori. You must be able to feed a hundred."

"Not quite that many, not indoors anyway, but lots. We'll have thirty tonight. That's a small crowd for us. Come, I'll introduce you to everyone. Vaughn, please get her something to drink. We've got eggnog or champagne or coffee or tea. Hot chocolate. All kinds of sodas."

"Champagne, definitely." Frankly, she wouldn't have turned down having her own bottle.

Dori took her through the crowd, making introductions. There were brothers and sisters and cowboys and herdsmen and other titles she couldn't remember.

"I'm going to leave you with my son Mitch's wife, Annie," Dori said, "while I tend to dinner."

"May I help?"

"I've had lots of help. We're down to the last bit, and everything's under control, but thank you."

Karyn took a sip of the champagne Vaughn had delivered to her.

"Quite a crowd, isn't it?" Annie asked. She seemed to be about the same age as Karyn, but she was blonde and curvier. Karyn noticed how Annie and Mitch kept each other in sight and smiled a lot.

Karyn was used to hordes, although the tone was not usually like this happy, congenial group. "A good-looking group, too," Karyn said. "The men are all ruggedly attractive, and the women are stunning, starting with the matriarch." She looked around. "I haven't met the patriarch."

"He's tending the beef outdoors. You can't miss him. The Ryder men were made from the same mold. He's just an older version. Fit and authoritative, and he loves Dori with his whole heart." Annie sipped from her mug of cocoa. "I hear you've been hired to paint Cass's portrait. Is that what you do for a living?"

Karyn tried not to roll her eyes. "I do lots of things. Mostly I'm a personal shopper. I live in Hollywood."

"Really? Dori didn't tell us that."

"I don't think she knows." Karyn wasn't sure how

much to say but decided to be as honest as possible. "We didn't get much of a chance to speak when we met."

"How did Vaughn find you?"

"He did some research and discovered me. What's your story?"

"I'm a farmer. I grow only organics."

"How long have you known Mitch?"

"We met last summer and got married in October."

Karyn keyed in on that. "That was quick."

"When it's right, it's right."

"Dinner's on," Dori shouted while ringing a small cowbell.

A dining room table was set for sixteen, with other smaller tables scattered here and there, most seating four. A long peninsula that separated the kitchen from the dining area was loaded with food—prime rib, a mound of baked potatoes with all the fixings, tortellini with pesto, the largest bowl of green beans Karyn had ever seen plus several kinds of salads.

On the far side of the kitchen, on a counter atop two dishwashers, were four pies and four plates stacked with cookies. There was good-natured shoving and insulting until everyone loaded their plates and found seats.

Karyn found herself at the dining room table next to Vaughn's youngest sister, Jenny, who was home from college.

"No prime rib?" Karyn asked.

"Vegetarian since I was fourteen."

Karyn stared at her plate, feeling uncomfortable

now, drawing a small laugh from the pretty young woman who looked remarkably like her mother.

"If it weren't for the meat eaters of the world, I would've had a very different life, one not nearly as wonderful. Please, eat your beef. It's just a personal choice for me."

Karyn took a bite of the best prime rib she'd ever eaten. She'd loaded her plate with a bit of everything, including cranberry Jell-O salad, a green salad with orange slices and almonds plus olives and pickles and carrot sticks. She was enjoying every bite.

"Leave room for dessert," Jenny said. "There's nothing better in the world than my mom's pies. Except for her cookies."

Conversation may have lagged a little when they first sat down to eat, but it picked up shortly. Karyn looked around. Everyone seemed to be smiling. And talking. And laughing. And kidding around.

Annie was right. The moment Jim Ryder appeared, Karyn had known who he was. It was how Vaughn would look in twenty years.

She sought out Vaughn, who was seated at the other end and across, near his mother and next to his sister-in-law, Annie. Everyone was relaxed, comfortable with each other. They'd welcomed her warmly. But she suddenly missed her formal parents, and her brother, like crazy. Their family dinners had never been big and boisterous like this, but they were *her* family, *her* memories, and she ached for them now. Especially now, when it might be different for her parents, not so sad. They'd gotten a tree....

She'd feared she would never be able to celebrate again, would never overcome the deep-down pain she now associated with Christmas. Maybe there was hope after all.

Tears pushed at her eyes. She whispered "Excuse me" to Jenny and tried to seem casual about leaving the room, when she just wanted to run—run far away from all the camaraderie and connection, so lacking in her life.

She found a bathroom, did her best not to slam the door shut, then sank onto the toilet and let the tears flow, hot and full of longing for her so special brother who had been everything to her, her leader, her protector, her fan. He'd never let her down.

Kyle had never mentioned Cassidy's mother, Ginger, which to Karyn meant she hadn't been special to him. What was she supposed to take from that? They'd always talked about their relationships, giving each other advice.

A light tapping on the door had Karyn grabbing tissues and swiping at her face. "Yes?"

"It's Vaughn. Are you all right?"

"Of course. I'll be out soon."

"All right."

She held a cold, wet washcloth to her face, but it didn't help enough, and she couldn't hide out for an hour.

Resigned, she opened the door. Vaughn was there,

leaning against the wall. He pushed himself upright, stared at her for a few seconds, then, without a word, pulled her into his arms. She'd thought she was done with tears, but that sparked a whole new batch.

"My brother died on Christmas Eve," she said against his shoulder, his strong, solid, comforting shoulder.

"I'm so sorry."

"Seeing all of you together, having fun, just triggered...I didn't know it was possible to miss someone this much. Every year it's hard. I was with my parents for Christmas when the men came up the walkway. I felt like someone had set me under a boulder then shoved it over on me. I crumbled. I—"

His arms tightened. She squeezed him, digging her fingers into his back. "I don't want to go back out there."

"I'll take you home."

"No. Cassidy needs to be here—with you. Just let me lie down in one of the bedrooms. When you're truly ready to go, come get me."

"Okay." Vaughn fought the urge to lift her into his arms and carry her, fought his instinctual urge to take care of her. He couldn't remember seeing someone cry like that, that deeply and mournfully. He guided her down the hall to his old bedroom, which hadn't changed much through the years. None of their rooms had. His mother preferred to keep them as they were when they each left for college. "This was my room," he said to Karyn, slipping into the adjoining bathroom he'd shared with Mitch and dampening a washcloth.

She'd already lain down, her shoes toppling against each other on the floor. He lifted an afghan from the foot of the bed and draped it over her. "Maybe you'd prefer to just spend the night here?"

"No." She didn't seem to have the strength to say more.

"Here's a washcloth and towel if you need them."

"Thank you. I'm sorry."

He almost leaned down and kissed her head, stopping himself at the last minute. In a strange way, he was glad he'd seen her break down, giving him an insight into her he never would've had otherwise. She'd cried a little at her apartment, but this was a full meltdown.

Vaughn returned to the dining room. The table was cleared and leftovers were being stored. After all these years, they had a routine of who did what. No one had to be assigned a task. The men always did the dishes. Vaughn grabbed a dish towel off the counter.

"Is she all right?" his mother asked.

"She's exhausted, I think. She drove up from L.A. today. Long drive, plus all these people." He shrugged.

"It seemed more than that. She's looked sad all night."

Vaughn weighed his answer. "Her family isn't like ours. She only had one brother. He was killed in Afghanistan three years ago today."

"Today? Oh, that poor girl." She wiped her hands on her apron. "Should I go talk to her?"

"I don't think so. She's lying down in my room. I

think she would be embarrassed to have you see her like that."

Dori put her hand on Vaughn's arm. "I have questions."

"I can see that, Mom, but not now, please. When I can, I'll tell you more." He reached around her and picked up a pot to dry, stopping the conversation.

Much later he noticed Cassidy's eyes drooping as his father gathered the children to sit on the floor and listen to him read *The Night Before Christmas,* a family tradition, the book from his childhood. Cass curled up in her granddad's lap, a sleepy smile on her face, as he read the long poem dramatically. The children were mesmerized.

"And to all a good night" was the cue for everyone to say their goodbyes. A flurry of activity followed, with lots of hugs and kisses. Vaughn carried his daughter to the truck, leaving his brother Adam to watch her while he got Karyn.

He tapped on the bedroom door, but she didn't answer. He crept inside and found her curled into a ball, her fists under her chin, asleep. He wished he could just leave her, but he knew she didn't want that, would feel too awkward in the morning, so he laid a hand on her shoulder and quietly said her name.

She woke instantly, looking confused for a few seconds. "What time is it?" she asked.

"Time to go home. Cass is in the truck already."

She whipped the covers back, slipped her shoes on,

climbed out of bed, then leaned over to straighten the bedding. He helped.

"How many people are still here?" she asked.

"Maybe no one but Mom and Dad and my sister Jenny. Everyone was taking off."

"I need to get my purse and thank your parents."

"All right."

She took a couple of steps then stopped. "I look horrible, don't I?"

Honestly, she looked like she'd been wrung through a wringer. "You look tired."

She sort of laughed. "That was kind—thank you."

His parents were on the porch saying goodbye to his other sister, Haley.

"Thank you for including me," Karyn said to his mother. "I'm sorry I conked out on you."

Dori pulled her in for a hug. Vaughn was afraid it would set Karyn off again, but she did okay.

"We'll see you tomorrow," Dori said.

"I'll try to stay awake. Good night, sir," Karyn said to Jim, shaking his hand. "You have a wonderful family."

"Appreciate it," he said.

Adam shut the back door of the truck as they approached. "She's out cold."

"Thanks. See you later."

The drive was quiet. No conversation, no music, and the weather crystal clear. When they reached his house, he carried Cassidy while Karyn teetered on those amazing high heels. They climbed the stairs together. Karyn opened Cass's door for them.

"Thanks."

"Thank you, Vaughn. You've been very thoughtful. Good night."

"Sleep in. We won't have to leave until eleven."

She nodded then disappeared into the guest room.

As he tucked his daughter into bed, his thoughts kept going to Karyn. He couldn't let himself get attached to her—he knew that for a fact. If she was Cass's aunt, she would be in their lives forever. If she wasn't related, this would be it, a one-time visit. They lived too far apart. She had a career in Los Angeles. His was here.

But he was attracted in a big way.

He wandered down the hall to his own room. He liked things neat and tidy, including his relationships. He compartmentalized them according to his need and how the other person filled it. He had women friends, including one he slept with now and then, but no one woman for everything. Maybe no one ever would. He tried to keep his needs to a minimum—all his needs.

"I wish I had a brother," Cass had said earlier, twisting his gut a little.

He'd like to give her a brother or two, maybe a sister also, but it had to be with the right woman this time. One who would stay forever and be happy at the ranch.

And he was sure that a personal shopper to Hollywood stars couldn't fill that role.

Chapter Five

"How do you walk in those shoes?" Cassidy asked Karyn the next morning as they were getting ready to go to the homestead for Christmas Day.

"Like this," Karyn said, walking across the living room and back.

Cass giggled. Karyn laughed too. She felt a thousand percent better this morning. She'd slept until ten, took a long shower, spent time on her hair and makeup, then dressed in blue jeans, a white sweater and high-heeled boots. Silent silver bells hung from her ears.

"Do you have lots of shoes?"

"I don't know for sure how many, but lots, yes," Karyn said. She knew it was more than a hundred. "I don't buy them all. People give me shoes frequently."

"Why?"

"Because they're movie stars and they can't wear them too many times in public."

"*Why?*"

"That's the way it is in Hollywood. Most of my clothes are hand-me-downs, too."

"Whose sweater was that?" Vaughn asked, coming into the room. He'd already emptied the tree of presents and loaded them in his truck to take with them.

"Gloriana Macbeth's."

His brows went up.

Karyn just smiled. Maybe she didn't fill out the sweater in quite the same way, but it fit well enough she thought as she checked him out, too. He looked like a rancher this morning in his Wranglers, western shirt, boots and hat, as if he would hop on a horse and go chase cattle or whatever it was they did. He also wore a suede jacket with a sheepskin lining, adding to the look in a casually fashionable way.

"Your hair is curly like mine," Cassidy said, cocking her head.

Karyn's heart skipped a beat. "It sure is."

"I hate my hair. It's too hard to put in a ponytail, and if I cut it short, I look like my friend Julie's poodle."

"Believe me, I know how you feel. I can show you a few tricks to make it easier if you want, although your dad may have to help you until you get good at fixing it yourself." Karyn looked at Vaughn, asking silent permission. He folded his arms and stared back.

"Yeah! Okay, Daddy?"

"Maybe. You know I have trouble with doing your hair."

"Pleeease?"

"We'll talk about it later. Are you ready to go to Grammie and Granddad's?" he asked.

"Ready!" She jumped up and ran to the door.

"Is everything okay this morning?" Vaughn asked as he and Karyn strolled behind the little girl.

"Yes, thank you." She'd decided not to be embarrassed about it.

"Is that a sketch pad?" he asked, gesturing toward her hand.

"I thought I'd capture some images today. Get some practice. That's okay, isn't it?"

"From what you told me, it's a very good idea."

She smiled. "This is a brand-new pad. Starting fresh. I really hadn't expected to end up at your house until the test results were in. I figured I'd drive around and find things to draw and then paint later, something I haven't done for a while."

"Did you factor in the temperature?"

"It never occurred to me, but I can sit in my car and work."

They climbed into the truck and buckled up.

"It's *Christmas,* Daddy!" Cassidy said from the backseat. "And I've been *nice.*"

"You have, indeed."

She looked out the window for a few seconds. "Do you think Santa will ever start bringing my presents to our house instead of Grammie and Granddad's? Could we put an arrow on our roof to point the way? He must be confused by all the buildings and gives up."

"That's a good idea, Cass. Maybe we can try that next year."

Karyn turned to look at her. She had the sweetest face, with bright, intelligent green eyes and a curious expressiveness. She was incredibly articulate for a six-year-old, but then she'd apparently spent most of her life around adults.

Only a few vehicles were parked near the house and just twelve people expected, family plus Karyn. She was looking forward to getting to know the Ryders individually.

She ran through their names in her head—Jim and Dori were the parents. Vaughn was the oldest, then Mitch, who'd recently married Annie. She had a ten-year-old son, Austin. After Mitch came Haley, Adam and Brody, all single. Then finally Jenny, a senior about to start her last semester in college.

Karyn stepped into the house and stopped. The enormous Christmas tree was encircled by brightly wrapped packages, many added since last night. Did everyone buy for everyone? she wondered.

"Merry Christmas, sweet girl," Dori said, opening her arms as Cassidy ran to her.

They spoke for a few seconds, then Cass raced off to greet everyone else. Vaughn kissed his mother's cheek, said something in her ear that made her smile, then followed Cass into the group standing by the big fireplace being tended by Brody.

"Welcome," Dori said to Karyn, giving her a hug. "Merry Christmas."

"Thank you. The same to you. And, yes, I feel better today," Karyn said before she was asked. "Much better. Vaughn was very helpful."

"That's our Vaughn. Helpful to the max."

The door opened behind her, and Mitch, Annie and Austin came in, the last to arrive. Annie carried a casserole covered with foil. "Tortilla breakfast casserole," she said. "If there's room, I'll put it in the oven to stay warm."

"Plenty," Dori said.

"May I help?" Karyn asked.

"You can open the oven door," Annie answered with a grin.

Haley and Jenny were putting the final touches on a fruit tray, Jim and Adam came through the back door carrying a platter of bacon and sausages they'd grilled outdoors and Vaughn and Mitch came looking for coffee. The kitchen felt like a swarm in a hive, with people weaving in and out and the chatter of conversation creating a buzz. It was a home, cozy and welcoming.

She wondered if they ever argued.

Of course they did, she thought, answering her own question. But they wouldn't hold onto their anger for long or carry a grudge.

Her parents had never argued, at least not in front of her and Kyle. Everything had been civil, always. But neither had their home been a joyous kind of place like this one. She was trying not to compare the two families, but it was hard not to.

However, she only knew the tip of the Ryder iceberg. On the surface they seemed perfect.

With Christmas music playing in the background, they gathered around the table for brunch. The two kids could hardly sit still. Most of the men had already put in a few hours on the ranch, working up an appetite. Karyn wouldn't have believed twelve people could consume so much food at one sitting, but there were few leftovers.

This time she was seated next to Vaughn, and although they weren't crowded at the huge table, she could almost feel his arm touch hers now and then. Which it didn't. Ever. But heat rose from him that she could feel, which both comforted and tingled. She enjoyed watching them all interact, but especially Vaughn, whose voice was calm and steady and whose words were often wryly funny.

He would be good in a courtroom, she decided. Good in a crisis.

The table was cleared but the dishes were left on the counter so that presents could be opened. Karyn curled in a big leather chair with her sketch pad. She wondered whether the "big" gifts would be given out first or last.

Most of the presents were practical—clothing or horse gear. There were gift certificates to nearby restaurants or for downloading books and music on electronic players. As the packages dwindled to almost none, Jim stood, getting everyone's attention, and asked Dori to join him. Her cheeks turned pink at all the attention.

Her sons teased her. Her husband took her hand and drew her close then passed her an envelope. "Merry Christmas, sweetheart."

She lifted the edge and slipped out the contents. "What? What's this? Hawaii? Are we going to Hawaii?"

"Yep." He beamed, proud of his surprise. "We leave New Year's Day."

"We haven't been on a vacation longer than a weekend in…twenty years."

"Then it's about time, don't you think? The boys'll manage everything okay for a week."

"Oh, honey! Leave it to you to plan a trip to Hawaii in a week, no less, and expect me to buy a tropical wardrobe." She laughed and hugged him.

Twenty years? Karyn thought as she sketched quickly, trying to capture the joyful look on Dori's face and the pleased-as-punch one on Jim's. Was it usual for all of them not to take vacations? Because of time? Money? Both? Karyn tried not to show her surprise. Everyone needed a vacation from their daily lives.

Except you've done the same thing...

The family hadn't settled down yet when Mitch passed his parents a small, wrapped box. Inside was a tiny white onesie with the words *I love my Grammie and Granddad* printed on it. Dori leaped up to hug Mitch and Annie and then Austin.

"When?"

"Early August."

Brody counted on his fingers. "Oh, man. That must've been some wedding night."

Mitch kissed his wife's temple. "It was."

Austin joined them, pulling off his plaid shirt to reveal his own T-shirt underneath: *Big Brother*.

Karyn wished she could capture the essence of the moment, the emotions, and fill in the rest later, but she couldn't sketch as fast as it all occurred. Her hand cramped, but she kept going, even after seeing how raw the images were. She was so unpracticed and amateurish. Maybe she would end up tossing everything.

"Okay, one more gift outside. Come on, Austin," Mitch said.

Everyone went out the front door, where two horses stood patiently. Austin took the steps slowly, a huge grin on his face. He looked at Mitch. "Mine?"

"All yours."

Karyn felt her own mouth stretch into a smile. She had no idea what breed the horse was, but it was a beautiful color, deep chestnut, with a white blaze down its face. Face? Was that right? And a black mane and tail.

The horses were already saddled. Mitch and Austin climbed aboard, waved and were off.

"Is this his first time?" Karyn asked Annie, who beamed.

"No. He's been riding for a few months now. He loves it. I, on the other hand, have a love/hate relationship with horses." She rested a hand on her still-flat abdomen. "And now I have an excuse not to ride. Nice bonus."

"You live on a ranch, but you don't want to ride? Can you get away with that?"

"I've got my farm, so I'm plenty busy. It's about twenty miles from here. We moved into Mitch's house on the ranch when we got married, but I work out there almost every day."

"I'd love to see your farm," Karyn said as everyone moved back into the house.

"You're welcome any time." She called over to her sister-in-law. "Jenny, since you're coming to the farm tomorrow, why don't you pick up Karyn and bring her along? Cass, too. Now that it's Christmas break, she and Austin—"

Cassidy let out a shriek as she spotted Vaughn carrying a brown, tan and white puppy with light blue eyes. Vaughn dropped to his knees in front of his daughter.

"Oh, thank you, Daddy! Thank you, thank you, thank you." She giggled as the puppy licked her face. "He looks just like Bo."

"Except this one's a girl," Vaughn said, placing the wiggly dog in her lap.

Again, Karyn wished she could sketch fast enough to capture the delight on her face, but she couldn't, so she just held her sketch pad to her chest and enjoyed watching.

"Who's Bo?" Karyn asked Annie.

"My son's Australian shepherd."

"Do I get to name her?" Cassidy asked her father.

"You do."

She held the puppy up, touching noses with the squirming bundle. "Belle. I'll call you Belle."

From his back pocket, Vaughn pulled out a leash,

which he hooked onto the harness the puppy already wore. Too young for a collar yet, Karyn guessed. "Let's take her for a walk."

The men all went outdoors with them while the women headed to the kitchen to clean up, Dori storing the few leftovers, her two daughters loading the dishwasher and Annie and Karyn washing pots and pans. Christmas music still played. They talked about the baby to come, Hawaii and how Austin seemed destined to become a cattleman. He'd taken to ranching as if born to it, which pleased his stepfather, Mitch, to no end, even though Annie would love for him to take over the farm someday.

"People have to choose their own paths," Dori said. "Hard as it may be for a parent to accept that. Look at Vaughn."

All the women nodded. Karyn frowned when she realized they weren't going to add to it. "What about Vaughn?"

"Oh." Dori looked around, then smiled. "I forgot you didn't know about him. It feels like we've known you forever."

Karyn was touched by her words.

"We knew Vaughn was different early on," Dori said. "Not that he didn't take to the land, but he was just so… studious. Always had his head in a book. And words? He loved words. He studied the dictionary, wanted to know the roots of words and their meanings, whether the origins were Latin or Greek. Then he'd teach us about what he learned while we ate."

"Lecturing, you mean. Bor-ing," Haley said like a teenager, then grinned. The pretty physical therapist was thirty-two and hadn't lived at home since college, Karyn had learned. She had her own small house in town, near the rehab hospital.

"Oh, don't be such a sister," Jenny said, bumping hips with Haley. "Vaughn never ducked out of work or responsibility. It's just that his dreams went beyond the ranch."

"He wanted the bright lights and big city," Dori said. "After law school he ended up in San Francisco and was there until three years ago. Made quite a name for himself as a litigator. Even as a boy he could talk anyone into anything, couldn't he, girls?"

"Why is he living here now?" Karyn asked while also mulling over the fact Vaughn could talk anyone into anything. She would have to be strong and not let him convince her of something she wouldn't be happy with.

"After Cassidy was born, he realized he wanted her to be brought up away from the city."

The Ryder women all looked at each other as if deciding how much to say.

"Anyway, that's one example of people choosing their own path," Dori said. "It's what Haley's done and what Jenny will do when she's done with college."

"Five more months. Yippee!"

So. They protected their own, Karyn thought. They didn't give her details of Vaughn's life with Ginger. She respected them for that.

"Well, girls, shall we start fixing dinner?" Dori asked, drawing laughs from everyone. "You think I'm kidding?"

They made lasagna and salad, putting both in the refrigerator for later, finishing just as all the men and Cassidy returned, the sleeping puppy cradled in Vaughn's arms.

Karyn was struck by the image, almost like a father holding a baby. It suited him. He had a paternal ease about him. He and Cassidy were a team, but he was always the parent. Karyn had many times seen single parents let their children rule the roost. Not Vaughn.

Because of that, Karyn knew he would want what was best for Cassidy—and surely that was to spend time with her aunt. Lots of time.

Stop counting on the fact Cass is Kyle's, Karyn told herself as forcefully as possible.

Hours later, well fed and talked out, everyone got ready to leave. Karyn passed out her sketches as her gift for including her in their family day. She laughed at her own attempts, calling them a little better than stick figures, but everyone seemed thrilled. She'd captured Jim stretched out on the floor helping Austin put together a remote-control helicopter and Dori trying to dance the hula, her face lit up. Karyn had caught each person in a special moment, including one with Mitch resting his hand on Annie's belly, their love palpable. She recreated Austin on his horse, Cassidy with her puppy asleep in her lap and a thoughtful Jenny and contented Haley as they curled up on a sofa talking leisurely.

Karyn caught Adam and Brody in rare moments, not teasing a sibling but sitting still and listening, eyes smiling.

And then there was Vaughn. He interested Karyn the most—or second most—so she started and eliminated several different sketches, trying to capture him dancing with Cassidy as a carol played in the background. He'd spun her in circles again and again, her face a sunbeam of delight, and at the end she curtsied and he bowed. Obviously they'd done this before. The bow and curtsy was what she'd sketched.

"How long will you stay?" Dori asked Karyn, walking to the truck with them.

"I'm not sure. It'll take as long as it takes," she said, smiling. "I suppose I'll be gone by the time you get back from Hawaii, if not before you leave." She studied Dori's face. "What you said about not having a vacation more than a weekend long…"

"Being a rancher is hard work. Daily work."

"Did you know that when you married him?"

"No, although he tried to tell me. I was a town girl, but I loved that man enough to take a rocket to the moon with him if he'd asked. I'm excited about the trip, but I love my life here. It doesn't matter where I spend my time as long as he's with me."

"You're quite an example."

"I'm not so sure about that."

"Really? All of your children seem content. Mitch, especially, is happy. Annie's there for the count," Karyn said.

"You're right. She's as steady as they come, and she has ambition. I think if you don't have something to do, something to strive for, it spills over into every relationship you have. You have to feel good about yourself first."

They'd almost reached the truck. "How about you, Karyn? Your job sounds glamorous on the surface, but is it really?"

"It can be. I've worked for some remarkable people. Most of them have been great."

"But there are exceptions?"

"Of course."

The puppy had been loaded into a crate for the drive home and set on the seat next to Cassidy, who cooed at Belle like a new mom with a baby.

"I'm not sure Vaughn realizes what he's gotten into by getting that pup," Dori said. "But Cass has been begging for one for years. It was time." She hugged Karyn. "I hope to see you again."

"I won't go without saying goodbye. Thank you again."

"Thanks for our sketches. We'll cherish them."

Karyn hugged Jim goodbye then climbed into the truck. They all were quiet during the drive home. It was seven o'clock. Clouds had moved in during the afternoon. It smelled like rain and brought back childhood memories with it, although it had often snowed on Christmas at home. It wasn't cold enough for snow tonight, even if the clouds opened up.

When they reached the house, it took a while to unload everything, get Cass ready for bed, start a fire in the living room and warm some cocoa. It looked like the perfect way to end the holiday.

Until Vaughn told Cassidy she couldn't keep the puppy in her bed.

Chapter Six

"But Daddy! She's going to be so lonely."

"Before you get upset, let me tell you why."

Cassidy crossed her arms and frowned but said nothing. Vaughn knew the look well. "You're right, sweetheart. She's going to be lonely because she's been with her mother and brothers and sisters since she was born, which is one reason why she'll be difficult during the night for a while, maybe even weeks. I have a teddy bear to put in the crate with her. We rubbed it all over her mother and the others to get their scent. That will help."

"The crate! She can't sleep in the crate all by herself."

"I know you think it's harsh, but she'll be okay. I'll be close by."

"I want her to sleep with *me*."

"I'm not saying she won't. But until she adjusts, this is best. Plus she'll need to be taken outside to pee several times during the night. Do you want to do that?"

"Yes, I do."

Out of the corner of his eye he saw Karyn cover her mouth against a smile.

"You'll have all day to play with her, Cass. Now, let's have a quiet few minutes in front of the fire before bed. Your hot chocolate's getting cold."

She flounced onto a floor cushion. Belle came bounding up to her, and soon she was giggling, crisis over. Before she'd even finished her drink, she was asleep.

"At least there won't be another scene," Vaughn said to Karyn as he lifted Cassidy into his arms to carry her upstairs. "Will you keep the puppy down here?"

"Of course."

He settled his daughter in bed, then sat beside her for a minute. It'd been a good Christmas, better than he could remember in a long time. There was no drama, like during the years with Ginger, and no loneliness, like the years since she'd left. He hadn't been lonely for her, but for someone to share the day, someone to wind down with.

Karyn had enjoyed herself, he was sure of that. Unlike last night, she was relaxed, helping out, fitting in. Her rough sketches had caught ephemeral moments. He particularly liked the one of his mother dancing the hula, looking young and vibrant. His father had surprised everyone with that vacation gift. Vaughn hoped they would be able to relax and enjoy their time away.

He kissed Cassidy's head, whispered good-night, then left the room. Unless Karyn was exhausted and wanted to go to bed early, they would have a couple of hours alone together. Would they be easy or awkward?

He headed downstairs.

"You are one lucky pooch," he heard her say. "You've landed in the best place possible. Open land, adoring kid, strict master. You've got it made."

"Strict master?" he repeated as he joined her in the living room. He went straight to the fireplace to stoke the logs. She sat in his big leather chair, cross-legged, her boots on the floor, the dog curled in her lap.

"That's a compliment," she said. "You'll make sure she's obedient. There's nothing better than a well-trained dog."

He looked over his shoulder at her. "Thank you. I guess."

She smiled, continuing to finger comb Belle's fur. "So, was that a rare scene for Cassidy or a normal one?"

"What? Her being stubborn?"

"Yes. And smart. If you hadn't asserted yourself as the one in charge, she could've gotten her way. She's bright enough to know when to back down."

"Naturally I think she's the world's most brilliant child. I figure she'll be quite a handful in years to come. But to answer your question, that was normal. She challenges me frequently. I think it's good. For now."

"Picture her as a teenager."

"Exactly." He put the poker into its slot on the rack then walked over to her to pet the puppy, aware that his fingers came close to touching her thighs with each stroke. "Belle. It's a good name for a dog."

His words were meant to divert himself from what was really on his mind—how Karyn had the perfect body, with curves in the right places, tempting him to touch for himself. He'd spent the day watching her, appreciating her grace and finding her incredibly sexy.

He saw how she'd watched his daughter with longing. He looked into her eyes now and saw a different kind of longing, one that matched his. Their attraction had come fast, would only intensify as they spent time together.

Or maybe not. Maybe they would be turned off by certain aspects of each other's personality.

He hoped. Because it wasn't a good idea at all to act on the attraction, not for either of them.

"You're a good daddy," she said now, quietly.

"Thank you. It's not always easy being mother and father."

"Exactly."

Vaughn pulled his hand away, hearing a velvet threat in the single word. They were at odds. Karyn wanted Cassidy to be Kyle's but also wanted Cassidy for herself, in effect, giving her a daughter and providing a mother figure. Vaughn wanted Cass to be Kyle's so that he would be done with his search and not have a biological father claiming her, fighting for her, but Vaughn also didn't want to share her with Karyn, who was available only from a long distance and who lived a different kind of life than what he wanted for his daughter.

"What are your plans if she turns out to be Kyle's?" he asked Karyn.

"Let's not jump the gun."

"You must have thought it through."

"I try not to." Belle hopped down from Karyn's lap and started sniffing the floor.

"Saved by the immature bladder," Vaughn said, grabbing the leash. "If you're hungry, feel free to fix yourself something. The refrigerator's full."

He escaped outdoors. Because Belle was twelve weeks old she was somewhat trained, the owner having kept her and most of the other pups so that they could be surprises for Christmas. Belle knew what she was expected to do outdoors, but that didn't stop her from wanting to sniff everything in sight, and Vaughn wasn't in a hurry to go back to the conversation he and Karyn had been having.

When he did go inside, he found her fixing a plate of cheese and apples, enough for two.

"I don't see how I could be hungry," she said. "But I am."

"Me, too."

"I figured. Do you have crackers?"

"In the cupboard over there."

She'd put her boots on. Even so, she couldn't reach the box of crackers in the cabinet. He pulled it down and handed it to her. Their hands touched briefly, and he remembered the way she'd felt in his arms last night when he'd comforted her.

"So, you're wearing Gloriana's sweater," he said, diverting his thoughts as she piled crackers in the middle of the plate.

"Half my wardrobe is from her. She's a difficult person to work for, but she surprises me with her generosity, too."

"Do you ever buy her something because you like it and hope you'll get it later?" He snagged a cracker and square of cheese from the plate.

"Well…"

"Mercenary."

"Guilty. It hasn't always worked out." She nibbled on an apple slice.

"Do you like your work?"

"Most of the time. Sometimes it just seems…frivolous. Especially since Kyle died. I feel like I should be doing something that matters more. Like I need to live life for both of us, and he had higher ambitions than I did, more important goals."

"Like what?"

"He had a degree in civil engineering, and he had dreams of working with the Peace Corps on roads and dams in third-world countries."

"Admirable."

"He was happiest doing something to help others. He was the most self-sacrificing person I knew."

"What were his flaws?"

"His flaws? Should we speak ill of the dead?"

"If we want to avoid putting someone on a pedestal. I'd like to know about him, not just because he might be Cass's father but because he's your brother, and you obviously adored him."

"I expect most sisters adore their big brothers." She leaned her elbows on the island countertop and smiled.

"So he was born first?"

"By three whole minutes." She cocked her head. "He was nice to everyone."

"Too nice?" he asked, hearing something beyond just an observation.

She shrugged.

"Did people walk all over him?"

"He got taken advantage of, yes. Was that Ginger's M.O.? Was she a user?"

"And a chameleon." He didn't want to talk about Ginger. She'd figured out right away how to bring out his protective instincts. She'd probably done the same with Kyle and every other man she'd met.

"Was your marriage terrible?"

"Not for the first couple of years." As long as they were living in San Francisco and she could shop all day, she was fine. As soon as they'd moved here—much against her wishes—she became a different person, probably her true self.

"Did she love Cassidy?"

He noticed Karyn didn't ask if Ginger had loved him. She'd probably figured that out for herself. Vaughn had been a means to an end for Ginger, that was all. "She wasn't very maternal. She dressed Cass up like she was her baby doll, constantly changing her clothes. Once Cass was old enough to assert herself a little and not be so completely dependent, Ginger lost interest. Then she left."

"I'd like to ask a personal question, even though it's none of my business—"

"Why did I marry her when she'd just given birth to another man's child?"

Karyn nodded.

"I thought I was in love." More important, he'd thought she needed him. He'd been raised to respect and protect women. He'd seen it all his life, the way his father was with his mother and sisters. There was an unspoken code, an expectation of a Ryder male. It hadn't taken much effort on Ginger's part to discover that about him—and use it.

"How did you meet?"

"She was a temp in my law office." He was done looking back, didn't need to be talking about her, ruining the first Christmas he'd enjoyed in years. "I'm going to take the dog out once more then go to bed. Feel free to stay up and enjoy the fire."

"I'm wiped out, too."

They put the food away. At the bottom of the staircase, they said good-night.

"I hope Belle doesn't keep you awake all night," Karyn said.

"Thanks. Me, too."

He crouched to attach Belle's leash but got distracted by seeing Karyn climb the stairs. Her designer jeans were a second skin, emphasizing her rear and not leaving a whole lot to his imagination. She didn't look back at him but wiggled her fingers over her shoulder when she reached the top of the stairs, letting him know she was aware of him watching.

"Well, pup," he said. "It should be an interesting few days."

Belle, being female, smiled mysteriously. Hell, even the dog seemed to know everything, while he felt as if he knew nothing at this point. He'd been trying not to compare Karyn to Ginger, but he couldn't help it. There were similarities. Both of them were flashy, although Karyn in a more tasteful way. She dressed for where she worked, the people she worked for.

The most worrisome comparison had to do with the speed with which everything was happening. It'd been that way with Ginger, too. Too much, too fast. He'd learned that Ginger had set him in her sights from the beginning, and maybe Karyn had, too. Was she pretending her attraction? Setting the scene for what she wanted if Cass was her niece?

Was it just his ego that he felt attraction from her?

He wouldn't be played for a fool twice.

The night before, Karyn had slept straight through, even being in a strange place, which was a testament not only to how tired she had been but also to how comfortable she'd been with the surroundings.

Tonight was a different matter altogether. She'd fallen asleep easily enough but awakened after a few hours unable to doze off again. The house was quiet. She'd heard the puppy whining and barking while she'd been getting ready for bed, but nothing after that. Karyn assumed the dog wasn't happy being crated.

Poor Vaughn. Maybe he should've gotten a rescue dog, one who came fully trained and who slept through the night, although it was fun for kids to grow up with a dog they'd raised themselves. Because Belle was a herding dog, Karyn wondered if she would be trained to herd cattle along with being a family pet. She wondered if Vaughn was involved in the day-to-day ranching operations. Did he ride herd—or whatever it was called?

Karyn stared at the ceiling until she couldn't lie there anymore. She ran a bubble bath, luxuriating in the warmth, then put her T-shirt and pajama bottoms back on. Still she wasn't sleepy, so she tugged her robe on, grabbed her sketch pad and quietly went downstairs to the living room, curling up in the big leather chair, a floor lamp on over her shoulder. She'd just opened her sketchbook when the front door opened.

Belle bounded in, straining at the leash. She barked once. Vaughn said, "Quiet," as he took off her leash then lifted her into his arms, apparently not taking the chance she would run off, thus making him chase her through the house.

"Having a rough night?" Karyn asked.

Vaughn spun toward the living room. "Looks like I'm not the only one," he said, the squirming dog trying to lick his face. He wore sweatpants, a sweatshirt and slippers.

"Are you feeling okay?" he asked.

"Yes, why?"

"Your cheeks are pink. Your hair looks wet."

"I'm not feverish. I took a bubble bath, hoping to—" She stopped as his gaze intensified.

"It didn't help, apparently," he said, putting the dog down. She raced over to Karyn and tried to jump into the chair, obviously happy when Karyn lifted her up.

"How many times have you taken Belle out?"

"Twice. I can stir up the embers and get the fire going if you want."

"I'm fine, thank you. I hope to go back to bed soon. Have you had any sleep?"

"Some. She's letting me know she's not happy about being by herself in the crate. She'll adjust." He gestured to her sketch pad. "May I have a look?"

She hesitated then finally relinquished it. "I need to flesh out a lot of them. Or toss them."

"I can't draw or sing, both of which I'd like to do," he said as he flipped through the pages, examining each drawing.

"There are kind of a lot of you," she said apologetically. "Or beginnings, anyway."

"I'm seeing that. Why?"

"You have an expressive face, especially with your family." She could easily stare at that face across the breakfast table for the rest of her life, she thought, then caught herself. "When you have your lawyer's face on, as you did when you came to see me in Hollywood, I only saw the business side of you. As you can see, I started a lot of drawings of Cassidy, too, and of you and her together."

He returned the pad. "I never thought about how different sketches are from photographs. You capture not just a moment but a series of moments, then combine them. That's talent."

His words pleased her beyond measure. "Thank you. I hope to get to that point."

They looked at each other for a few long seconds. Karyn's heart began to pound.

"I should get the dog crated and try to sleep," he said hesitantly, as if waiting for her to say otherwise.

"I should try, too." Belle had fallen asleep in her lap. She slipped her arms under the dog and lifted her toward Vaughn. Their hands brushed. It was all Karyn needed to acknowledge what was fast becoming a craving. She couldn't remember ever feeling this much this soon for anyone. Could she trust those feelings? She knew she was vulnerable right now. Was that what was driving her?

"Good night again," Vaughn said.

"Night."

Karyn waited until he was out of sight before she stood, then changed her mind and sat down again. She opened her sketchbook, looking for a particular drawing. When she found it she picked up her pencil to expand on it, to fill in the details. Vaughn was seated on a sofa, his arms stretched across the back, his ankles crossed. Relaxed and utterly sexy, he'd been watching Mitch and Annie slow dancing. His shirt had pulled tight over a flat abdomen and across a broad chest. Karyn sketched the sweet spot where his Wranglers bunched below his belt buckle. He would have a horseman's thighs, too, strong and muscular.

She closed her eyes and blew out a long, slow breath. She had a good imagination, and it was on overdrive picturing him naked. His body would be an endless delight to explore.

Karyn traced a finger over the sketch, down his face, his chest, his abdomen and beyond. She'd love to paint him in the nude, his muscles smooth and toned, especially his tight rear. If she were a sculptor, she'd want him as her subject. She'd take her time, too, lots and lots of time to get it right. He would be her muse, her manly muse. She'd have a bed handy so they could take frequent breaks and enjoy each other's bodies.

He would caress her, kiss her everywhere....

"Wow," she whispered. When she opened her eyes, he was there, standing in front of her. Her breath caught in her throat. She felt her face heat up. Could he read her thoughts?

"Wow, what?" he asked, but he had to know already, especially because her pad was open to the sketch of him she'd been working on.

He crouched, bringing himself eye to eye with her. "I thought you were going to bed."

"I wanted to finish this first."

He turned the pad around. "Is that how you see me?"

"Do you find fault with it?" Oh, he was so close.

Close enough to steal a kiss before he could back away, if she dared.

"You make me look younger than I feel."

"A little bit of gray at the temples doesn't age you." She brushed at the gray with her fingers then let them drift over his ears and down his jaw.

He drew a quick breath. "We can't do this," he said roughly, capturing her hand, holding it.

"Do what?"

"Any of this. It's too complicated. We barely know each other."

He was right, of course. What had gotten into her? It would be crazy—

"When we have the test results and know what we're dealing with, then we can make conscious, thought-out decisions," he added.

"You talk too much, cowboy lawyer."

He laughed softly and stood. It was obvious he wasn't wearing briefs and just as obvious that he wanted her. She hadn't overestimated him, not in the sketch and not in her mind.

She didn't want him to reject her, nor did she want to confuse their situation, so she got up from the chair and left, not looking back once, knowing he watched her, excited by the idea.

And hopefully leaving him wanting more.

Chapter Seven

"Are you sure you don't mind?" Karyn asked Vaughn the next morning as they were eating breakfast. "I should be doing something. Sketching?"

He gave her a look that seemed to indicate his doubt. At least he now believed what she'd told him about not being capable of pulling off a portrait of a girl and her horse. How he would explain to the family the lack of a finished product would be interesting.

"You'll enjoy Annie's farm," he said. "I don't expect you'll spend the whole day, so there'll be time after you get back. Cass loves to go to the farm."

"Yes! It's so much fun." Cassidy swirled her last bite of pancake in maple syrup and stuffed it in her mouth. "Belle can visit Bo. He can teach her how to get the chickens in their coop."

"Not yet. She has one more vaccination to get before we should let her run free." He carried his dishes to the sink. "I've got work to do this morning myself, so you going to the farm is fine."

Karyn joined him at the sink. "Jenny won't arrive for a few more minutes. I'll do the dishes."

"It won't take me long. Maybe you should put something else on your feet."

Karyn looked down. "These are my work boots."

He laughed.

"They are. They only have a three-inch heel." She hadn't known what to expect after the tension of last night, but he acted as if it hadn't happened.

"I want my hair up like yours," Cassidy said.

Karyn looked to Vaughn for approval. He shrugged.

"Okay. Go brush your teeth, then come to my room."

Cassidy raced up the stairs. Vaughn put a hand on Karyn's arm, delaying her from following.

"You're not planning on sharing why you're really here with Jen or Annie, are you?"

"Of course not."

He released her, but she could still feel his heat on her arm.

"Were you able to go back to sleep?" he asked.

"Surprisingly, yes."

"Good."

She waited a little longer because it seemed like he wanted to say something.

"Is that all?" she asked.

"Yes. No." He cupped her face. "I thought I could

hold back from you. I was wrong. I couldn't get you out of mind all night."

He watched her eyes as he came closer, maybe waiting for her to say no or step back. She moved toward him. He brushed her lips with his, tasting of maple syrup.

"Mmm," she said. "Good morning."

Instead of smiling, he looked more serious than ever. At least he didn't say it'd been a mistake.

"I should get upstairs—"

He pulled her tight and gave her a kiss more reminiscent of bedtime than morning. She slid her arms around his neck. He wrapped his around her waist and dragged her against him.

"Karyn? Where are you?"

She pushed away from him, touching her fingers to her lips, then to his. His expression was fierce, his jaw like iron. He didn't like that he was attracted, she realized. Not one bit.

"I'm coming, sweetie," she called out. She made herself climb the stairs at a regular pace instead of racing up, as if running away. She wasn't running away. She wanted to stay right where she was.

Cassidy leaned on the bathroom counter and watched Karyn brush her teeth. She hadn't spent a lot of time around little girls, but she thought it was normal, part of the learning process, to watch what adults did.

"What do you call your hairstyle?" Cassidy asked.

"A messy bun."

Cass flashed a grin. "My hair is always messy."

"Mine, too. I also do the messy ponytail and the messy braid. Can't help it. Those curls just love to do their own thing. You don't ever brush your hair, do you?"

"Nope. It makes it fuzzy."

"Exactly. C'mere." She finger combed Cassidy's hair into a bun high on the back of her head, twisted it, wrapped it with a hair band, gave it another twist, then wrapped it again. "Voila!"

Cass looked in the mirror. "I look just like you!"

Karyn's stomach clenched. She didn't. Not really. Just her hair looked like Karyn. Wishful thinking wouldn't change that. Karyn didn't see herself—or Kyle—in Cassidy's features.

"It'll keep your hair out of your eyes," Karyn said. "Although it would be hard to wear a hat. Do you usually?"

"When I'm riding my pony. It's red."

"Jen's here!" Vaughn called up the stairs.

Vaughn did a double take as they came downstairs, but Jenny didn't seem to notice anything out of the ordinary.

"You look…seven or maybe even eight, missy." Jenny turned her in a circle.

"Oh, auntie," Cassidy said, but Karyn could tell she liked being told that.

"Could we have a one-on-one soon?" Jenny asked Vaughn. "I've got some business questions for you."

"Anytime, sis. I'm not going anywhere until after New Year's Day."

"Thanks."

Sis. Kyle had called Karyn that, too. The Ryder siblings were lucky to have each other.

The drive to The Barn Yard, as the sign outside Annie's property proclaimed it, took about twenty minutes, the landscape along the way mostly open fields. For grazing? Karyn wondered. Or hay?

An Australian shepherd barked a greeting as they pulled into the driveway then the yard in front of a small farmhouse. An old barn and even older shed took up space, as did three large structures that looked a little like Quonset huts.

"High tunnel greenhouses," Jenny said, seeing where Karyn was staring. "She can grow year-round."

"Welcome!" Annie waved as she approached. Cassidy ran up to her for a hug then joined ten-year-old Austin in the closest greenhouse. "Bo, down. Sorry. He behaves well for Mitch, but he knows I'm a softie."

She gave Karyn's feet a look. "I have boot envy. And the shoes you wore on Christmas Eve? The ones with the rhinestones? Only in my wildest fantasies."

"They'd be in my wildest fantasies, too, except, as I explained to Cassidy, my clients often give me shoes and clothing when they tire of them. I've bought very little for myself in years."

They moved toward the first high tunnel. Annie explained about her winter crops, the broccolini and colored cauliflower, and her year-round crops of baby lettuces, specialty potatoes and other produce.

"I got my organic certification a couple of months

ago, and I'm building a steady business with restaurants and markets. I've had some incredible help along the way. Even if I hadn't met Mitch, I would be on the path to sustaining myself here."

"I know very little about farming, but it seems like it would be so hard. I know you're dependent on the weather and the price of crops and insect invasion," Karyn said.

"All that and then some. Why don't we all go inside? The kids will be fine. Austin is very responsible. I gave him some cookies to share with Cass before they get dirty."

The outside of the house was deceptive. It seemed a hundred years old, but inside it was remodeled and updated, especially the kitchen. "Ignore the mess," Annie said. "Brody and Adam are living here for now. They're not world-class housekeepers."

Jenny shook her head. "Some things never change."

They sat at the kitchen table and shared tea, cookies and conversation. Karyn enjoyed Annie, a no-nonsense woman who loved her family and her farm. From the number of times she rested her hand on her abdomen, Karyn knew how much Annie looked forward to having her baby.

"Austin seems to be happy you're pregnant," Karyn said.

"He is, but I know they won't necessarily be close since there'll be an eleven-year age difference between them."

"They will be close until he leaves home," Jenny

said. "Then it'll strengthen again later. At least that's been my experience with my siblings. We've talked about it. I'm super close to Vaughn now, yet there's seventeen years' difference. He's in touch with me a lot. We even talk on the phone, not just text or email. He makes me do that."

She scrunched up her nose, but Karyn could tell it meant a lot to her.

"He's my mentor," Jenny said. "I count on him."

"He does seem very reliable," Karyn said.

Jenny laughed. "His middle name. Along with a slew of others, like orderly, organized, regimented. I could go on. It's what also makes him a good lawyer. So, Annie, how about finishing the tour? I've only been here once before—for the wedding. You've made changes since then."

"I've become more like Vaughn, organized and regimented," Annie said. "But that's what's needed here if I want to succeed."

The women headed to the front door. A pickup was coming up the driveway. "It's Win Morgan," Annie said, then looked at Karyn. "His father was trying to buy my land, and Win used to drop by to smooth talk me now and then. I preferred Mitch's kind of talk," she said with a wink.

"Um, I'm going to use your bathroom," Jenny said. "I'll catch up with you."

Karyn decided that if Win Morgan wanted to head to Hollywood, he would be named Sexiest Man Alive every year. He was probably twenty-five or so, with brown hair, brown eyes and a killer smile. She bet he would photograph so gorgeous and sexy that—

"Win," Annie said, not quite cool but not completely welcoming either.

He touched his hat. "Annie."

"This is Karyn Lambert. She's visiting."

Again he touched his hat. "Ms. Lambert."

"What can I do for you, Win?" Annie asked.

"We're fixin' to throw a New Year's Eve party at the ranch."

"And you're inviting the Ryders?" Annie asked sweetly.

The tension between them was fascinating to Karyn. A family feud or a personal one?

"Would you all come if we asked?" Win asked.

"I'm a Ryder by marriage, so I can't answer that, but I'd guess it'd be no."

He nodded. "My sister, Rose, wanted to know if you could sell us some lettuce and potatoes, whatever you've got ready. I know you supply businesses these days more than anything else, but Rose likes to use organically grown when she can."

"How many people are you feeding?"

"About twenty."

"I can do that. Have Rose email me through my website or give me a call. We can come up with numbers. You can pick it all up the day you need it."

"Thank you much." He took a few steps toward his truck then turned around. "You have a good Christmas?"

"We did, thanks. Did you?"

"It was okay. Hasn't been the same since Mom passed. I suppose your whole family gathered?"

"Yes, everyone."

"Jenny home from college?" His voice rose a little in the asking.

"For a couple of weeks, yes. Do you want me to say hi?"

"Nope, thanks. Just curious." He turned on his heel.

"Like heck you're just curious," Annie said as his truck disappeared. "It's not the first time he's asked about her, and since she made a beeline for the back of the house when she saw it was him, I'm betting there's something going on there."

"Is that why you didn't tell him she was here?"

"I believe in the sanctity of the sisterhood." She gestured toward the road. "There's something about him. He seems easygoing, but there's something deeper going on, a tension I can't figure out."

Jenny joined them.

"Win asked about you," Annie said, then headed toward one of the high tunnel greenhouses they hadn't toured yet, the kids and dogs joining them. "Come see what we're doing."

"I need to come back with my sketch pad," Karyn said as they were getting ready to leave a while later.

"Anytime," Annie said, giving her a hug. "Forget the sketches. I'll put you to work, boots and all."

The drive back to Ryder Ranch was too short. Karyn wanted to think about all she'd learned since she arrived, how differently the Ryders lived. She'd never given much thought to where her food came from. She tended to eat on the go or at restaurants. Ryder Ranch operated as an organic, humane business, a term she'd never heard of in reference to raising beef cattle.

Her eyes were being opened to a different world.

Jenny didn't just drop them off at Vaughn's house. She came in and met with him in his office while Cassidy played with the puppy and Karyn moved the kitchen table so that Cass could be by the window to sit for sketches.

"Remember, I want to wear sparkly shoes for the painting," Cass said, then took a bite of cookie.

"Shouldn't you have your riding clothes and boots on? That's what your dad, aunts and uncles are wearing in their portraits."

"But it's *my* picture."

There would be an interesting discussion between father and daughter about that, Karyn thought.

"I have a loose tooth." She wiggled a bottom front tooth. "Granddad says he's going to tie a string to it and have my pony pull it out." Her eyes went big and round at the idea.

"Do you think he means it?"

Cassidy frowned. "He wouldn't ever hurt me."

"So, he's just teasing you."

"Whew!"

Karyn smiled. She was a lively child, talkative and sweet and strong-minded. "How do you think you should wear your hair for the portrait?"

Cass squinted thoughtfully. "I think I should wear it down, like I usually do, because then it will look like me."

"Good thinking." Karyn penciled in a few lines on her sketch pad.

"Wait! My hair is up."

"I'm just doing what's called preliminary work. I'll do quite a few sketches before we start on the real thing." *Like maybe a hundred so I don't have to actually try to paint you.* "So, tell me about your pony."

"My daddy says she's a horse not a pony, but I don't think he knows."

"What's her name?"

"My Little."

Karyn grinned.

"Daddy calls her an old lady 'cause she doesn't move very fast. Pretty soon I'll get a new horse that'll run and run and run."

"How old will you be when that happens?"

"Maybe seven. We'll give My Little to Uncle Mitch and Auntie Annie's new baby."

"Can you sit up a little straighter, please? Thanks. I'd never been to a cattle ranch until this trip. What do you like about growing up here?"

"I like being with my daddy and my grammie and granddad. And everyone!"

"What do you think of the cattle?" Karyn started working on her eyes. She had the longest lashes.

"I dunno. They're pretty quiet most of the time."

"Do you play any sports?"

"Soccer. I'm the goalie. I have quick reflexes. That means I see the ball coming and block it fast. I only cried *once* last season." She looked proud of that fact.

"Why? Did you get hurt?" Karyn was tempted to put her pad aside and just have a conversation.

"No. We *lost.*"

Karyn compressed her lips for a second so she wouldn't laugh. "You mean you only lost one game the whole season?"

Cassidy nodded. "And it wasn't my fault."

"What happened?"

"That silly Marie Claire's bow came untied so she stopped to fix it. She was wide open for the shot."

"Well, you wouldn't have wanted her to trip and fall down, would you?"

"It was her *hair* bow." She folded her arms and huffed.

"Time to get over it, Cass," Vaughn said, joining them in the kitchen. "That was months ago."

"We *lost,* Daddy!"

"No one wins every game in life." He came up behind Karyn and looked at her sketch. She felt him all along her back even though he wasn't touching her. "Being a good sport matters, too."

"Are we done yet?"

"Sure," Karyn said, sorry that the conversation was ending. She'd learned a lot about Cassidy in just one sitting.

"She wants to wear sparkly shoes for her portrait,"

Karyn said to Vaughn after Cassidy left with Belle at her heels. "Does that mean I'm a bad influence?"

"You're something," he said, sitting in Cassidy's chair. "She has good role models, but you're really different."

"Is that good or bad?"

"Neither. It just is. I was thinking I'd ask Mitch, Annie and Austin over for pizza tonight. Sound good?"

"Don't want to spend time alone with me, hmm?" she asked.

He put his lawyer's face on. "I thought you would enjoy the company."

"Oh, this is for *me*?"

"I'm a thoughtful guy."

She laughed, then she leaned forward. "You don't want to be alone with me." In fact, he hadn't seemed able to stop himself from kissing her, had given in to that desire that morning. Since she wanted to be kissed again, she hoped he would lose control again very soon. Like now.

He rubbed a loose curl between his fingers. "Maybe."

Triumph mixed with trepidation in Karyn's mind. It was exciting to think she could attract a man like Vaughn, but the consequences of that attraction could be devastating. All she knew for sure was she hadn't felt this alive since Kyle had died.

And she didn't want it to end.

"I met Win Morgan at Annie's today," she said, setting her sketch pad aside.

"What was he doing there?"

"Placing an order for vegetables for a New Year's Eve party." She cocked her head. "I take it there's an issue between the Ryders and the Morgans."

"Going back to the gold rush, more than 150 years. Both families have ranched here since then, with the same problems. We both sold off land, had to, but we've been buying back for about forty years now, competing against each other for dominance. It's gotten a little cutthroat at times."

Karyn wondered even more about Jenny and Win, but she wouldn't be unfaithful to the sisterhood by asking Vaughn directly about them. "The families don't mix, I gather."

"Not on purpose." Vaughn shrugged. "We end up at the same charity events, things like that. It's kind of an unwritten rule that we don't mingle. Win's father is more rigid than my dad and has gotten worse since his wife died last year."

So, star-crossed lovers, maybe? Win had asked about Jenny, and Jenny had made herself scarce. There was a story there.

Karyn loved a good mystery.

She hoped she could get to the bottom of it before she had to leave.

Chapter Eight

Mitch and Austin came by early the next morning, way too early, Karyn thought as she entered the kitchen at six o'clock, having been awakened by laughter. She'd thrown on some clothes, sighed at her hair as she twisted it into a quick knot, then brushed her teeth. She joined the group.

They were going to ride fence, whatever that meant, and Cassidy had been invited along. Mitch's saddlebags were filled with supplies to repair barbed wire. Austin's bags held a portable breakfast Annie had put together. Cassidy would carry thermoses of hot chocolate and coffee.

"How long will you be gone?" Karyn asked.

"Can't predict," Mitch said. "Adam and Brody are

coming, too, so we'll be pretty efficient. Hours, anyway. They've got our lunch with them."

Karyn eyed Cassidy, who was giggling with Austin. She could sit in the saddle for hours without complaining? Karyn was pretty sure she couldn't say the same of herself.

"Everyone has fresh batteries for their walkie-talkies?" Vaughn asked.

"And spares," Mitch answered, then gave him a steady look. "You were younger than Cass when you first rode fence."

"I know. It's just…"

"I get it, Vaughn. I do. I'll take good care of her. We all will. She's been begging to do this, you know. It'll either cure her of the desire or give her a taste for more."

Vaughn's concerned gaze shifted to his daughter.

"Why don't you just go along?" Karyn asked.

"I'd be expected to repair fence."

His dry answer had her laughing. She didn't believe he ever shirked responsibility at any level.

They all walked outside. When Cassidy was in the saddle, Vaughn said, "You do everything your uncles tell you, no question, no argument."

"Okay, Daddy."

"And don't ask them to come home early. They have a job to do. They can't come back until it's done."

"O-*kay,* Daddy. Can we go now?"

He watched until they were out of sight. Karyn rubbed her arms, trying to stay warm in the cold morning air. It wasn't icy, but the skies were thick with clouds, not allowing any sunshine through. That hardly mattered, though, because it was barely past sunrise.

"Is there coffee made?" she asked, breaking into whatever he was thinking.

"Yes." He started up the stairs. "I'll get a fire going, too."

"Not on my account. I'm going to load my car and go scout locations to draw and take some pictures."

"Okay."

"Is this the first time she's gone on horseback without you?"

"No, but never as far as they'll go today."

"Do you do ranch work? I mean, on horseback? I know you're the lawyer for the corporation."

"I help out occasionally, especially during roundup, calving and haying." They entered the kitchen. He grabbed two mugs and filled them while she got the creamer from the refrigerator. "I generally ride daily. It clears my head."

"Do you have an office other than here?" She added cream to both mugs then stirred them before handing him his.

"No. I'm the attorney for forty-three farms and ranches, but I go to them or work by phone or internet. I do some family law, too, and consulting for my old firm as a strategist."

"Sounds like you have a full plate." She sipped her coffee, eyeing him over her mug.

"I prefer it. I like working from home, too. I quit

when Cass gets out of school, then pick it up again after she goes to bed."

"Does that leave you time for a social life?" She tried to sound mildly interested, but he saw through her casualness.

"On occasion. How about you?"

"Not for a while."

He seemed to be waiting for more, but she decided to remain mysterious. For a long time she'd felt as if she had nothing to offer a man emotionally. But ever since she'd met Vaughn—

"Are you hungry?" he asked.

Starved. For you. "What are you offering?"

Vaughn studied her, trying to decide whether she was talking about food or him. "A veritable feast."

Her eyes took on some sparkle. "Veritable, huh? You must have an extensive menu, I guess."

"From appetizers to dessert. À la carte or full meal." He kept his gaze directly on her, letting her know he wasn't really talking about food.

Her breathing changed, shortened.

He leaned a little closer. "The chef is also willing to entertain special orders."

"What if I ask for a cowboy lawyer over easy?"

He moved around the island, took her mug and set it down. He settled his hands on her hips. "Over hard's more my specialty."

She looped her arms around his neck, bringing her body against his. "I'll take one from column A and two from column B, please."

He wanted to take it slow, had planned to if he ever got the opportunity to kiss her again, but she was anxious and willing in his arms, and he wanted her. She had such soft lips, and her mouth was warm and wet as she made throaty sounds of need, the vibration reaching him, arousing him. He curved his hands over her rear, cupping her, lifting her, pressing his open mouth to her neck as she arched back, allowing it.

"I could lay you on this island and make a feast of you," he said, low and harsh, need driving him to sit her on the counter and shove his hands under her sweater, feeling the satin and lace covering her breasts, firm and full and tempting.

"Vaughn." Her voice shook. "We can't. You know we can't. I'm sorry. I shouldn't have teased you. Or teased back. It's too complicated."

He stayed put, keeping himself close.

"I want you," she continued. "Passionately. But it could cause too much harm down the road."

She was right, of course. He shoved away and walked toward the refrigerator, needing to do something, and stared into it without really seeing anything. "What if we don't sleep together but just make out a lot?"

She laughed, although it was more of a shudder than a true laugh. "Do you think we could do that?"

"I'm willing to try. I enjoyed the hell out of that, Hollywood." He used the nickname more as a reminder to himself of who she was, who she would always be, where she lived.

"It might work for teenagers, but adults?" she asked, skepticism in her voice.

"We won't get many opportunities anyway. People drop in regularly without warning. And Cass will be here most of the time, too. I'm serious. What do you think?" He straightened, looked at her. "Stolen pleasures? Think of the anticipation."

She blew out a breath. "We can try."

He glanced out the window and saw a horse and rider approaching. "My father's coming."

Startled, she fluffed her hair and checked her clothes. "Does he come by a lot?"

"Most mornings. He takes his second cup of coffee here."

"Do I look okay?"

She looked like she'd been kissed long and hard. "You look fine."

"Okay. Okay."

"Just one thing, Karyn."

"What?"

"I need to know what color your bra is."

"Why?"

"I know what it looks like by feel. I just need to add the color into my memory."

"White. It's white."

He smiled. He could hear his father coming up the steps. "Liar."

Her mouth pursed. "Black."

"Good try, but still a lie. Sexy but not you."

She sighed as a knock came on the front door then opened.

"Morning, son!"

Vaughn still waited her out.

"Fuchsia, okay?" she said in a low rush. "It's fuchsia."

"Matches your cheeks." He grinned then called out, "In the kitchen, Dad."

His father hesitated for a moment when he spotted Karyn, who was hiding behind her coffee mug.

"Mornin', Karyn."

"How are you, Jim?"

He eyed her thoughtfully, a smile hovering. "It's a good day."

Vaughn had already poured him a mug. He passed it to his father. "You're later than usual."

"It's your mother. She's in a tizzy about vacation clothes, is poundin' the keyboard. I tried to help, but she just gave me the glare. You know the glare?"

"Intimately."

"I could help," Karyn said, looking relieved and excited to get away at the same time. "I could get her some really good deals through my contacts. Have them shipped overnight. If you think she wouldn't mind, you could call and let her know I'll be on my way and to wait for me."

"She won't mind. Jenny stayed in town with her sister last night, so she's alone in this," Jim said, reaching for the kitchen phone. "Thanks. I think you just saved my hide."

"My pleasure. Tell her I'll be over as soon as I've showered." She raced from the room.

"You haven't had breakfast," Vaughn called after her.

"I'll live!"

"You gonna bite your nails the whole time Cass is gone?" Jim asked as he punched a speed-dial button.

"And ruin my manicure? Hardly."

His father laughed. "Hey, honey, Karyn says she can help you shop, even get you some discounts....She'll be there in a little bit. And she hasn't eaten breakfast yet....Good. Bye."

He hung up the phone. "That'll give her something to do while she waits."

Vaughn went about fixing his own breakfast— toaster waffles, a banana and precooked sausage he kept in the freezer.

"How's the portrait comin' along?" Jim asked.

"Slowly. It's hard to get Cass to sit still, plus with the holidays and all. You know."

"Does that mean Karyn will be here for a while?"

"It's open-ended." He nuked the sausage and dropped the waffles into the toaster.

"Seems like a nice gal."

"If you have a point to make, Dad, just put it out there."

"It's just...well, she's another city girl, isn't she?"

"She's here to paint Cass's portrait." *We hope. At some point.*

"You tryin' to tell me there's nothin' goin' on between you? 'Cause it didn't look that way to me. That girl's cheeks were as pink as a cow's tongue."

Vaughn laughed. "Now *there's* an image."

"I'd like to see you married again, no doubt about it," his father said seriously. "There are lots of local girls, women, who'd be happy livin' here."

"That's a pretty big leap you just made with regard to Karyn. I barely know her." Vaughn focused on the meal he was fixing so that he didn't have to look at his father. He was more than a little attracted to Karyn, and not just her body. She had a depth he hadn't anticipated, and Cass had taken to her right away. It could spell big trouble down the road.

"I knew I would marry your mom the first day I met her. It took a little convincing to get her to be a rancher's wife, but I can be pretty persuasive when I want to be."

"You don't have to tell me that." Vaughn filled his plate then sat at the kitchen table. His father topped off his mug and joined him. "Are you looking forward to your vacation, Dad?"

"Not sure I'm gonna know what to do with all that relaxation time, but yeah. I shouldn't have waited this long to take your mother away. If this works out well, we'll do it more often. Mitch wants more responsibility. It'd be a good way to give it to him. I'm still waitin' to discover what roles Adam and Brody will have."

"They know they can't be boss, not with Mitch here. Maybe they'll end up at other spreads. Would you be okay with that?"

"Not really. I put Adam in charge of the new solar

project we're installing. He seems happy with his place here. As for Brody? It's anyone's guess, but I sure would like to see him stay on at Ryder Ranch."

The sound of footsteps coming down the staircase stopped their conversation. Karyn stepped into the kitchen looking calm and stunning. She was wearing her normal high-heeled boots with what she called skinny jeans, plus a white lace top with a red cardigan over it, the edges ruffled. She looked longingly at Vaughn's almost empty plate.

"I'll probably go take pictures when I'm done," she said. "I have no idea how long I'll be."

"Have you got a map? You know we don't get cell coverage here, except by satellite."

She patted her purse, a large zebra-striped bag. "Got the map. See you."

Her scent reached Vaughn as she whisked herself away.

"Vanilla," his father said.

"What?"

"She's got vanilla perfume on. She's figured out what a man likes."

"What's that?"

"A woman who bakes—or smells like she does."

Vaughn laughed. He took his plate to the dishwasher. As he did, Belle got out of her dog bed and stretched, having slept the whole morning. Which was no surprise because she'd been up most of the night.

He grabbed her leash. "Let's go out, Belle."

She wriggled and yipped.

"Like having a newborn," his father commented, joining them as they went outside.

"Changing diapers in a nursery is much better than being outdoors in the dead of winter."

His father mounted up. "I don't think I'll show my face at home for a while."

"A sound idea."

"Thanks for the coffee. Maybe next time I'll call first."

Vaughn opened his mouth to respond, but his father whipped his horse around and took off at a canter.

A few minutes later Vaughn settled at his computer. Email was down to a few but would pick up again after New Year's when everyone got back to business. He checked his spam folder, saw the subject heading "Ginger Donohue" and clicked on it, although he didn't recognize the name of the sender, Jason Humphreys.

Dear Mr. Ryder,
This is an awkward email to write, but it's necessary. I heard you were looking for names of men who dated Ginger seven years ago. That would include me. You can call me and we'll discuss. I admit to being curious, having made a guess about it already.
Sincerely,
Jason Humphreys

He listed an address in Seattle and a phone number.

Vaughn stared at the screen, then moved the email into his inbox and walked away from the computer.

It was too early to call, which meant he had lots of time to stew instead.

And stew he would. Because this could change everything.

Karyn didn't even have to knock. Dori pulled open the door before Karyn had reached the steps.

"Where's your shining armor?" Dori asked.

Karyn relaxed for the first time since Vaughn's father had shown up earlier. "I left it in the barn with my trusty steed. It would've been hard getting into the car wearing it."

"It's difficult being a heroine in this modern world." Dori hugged her. "Breakfast first. It's all ready."

"*Now* who should be wearing shining armor?"

"A little bird told me you might be hungry."

"Tell Jim thank you." She took a seat on a kitchen stool as Dori opened the oven and pulled out a plate piled with country fried potatoes, bacon, scrambled eggs and a biscuit. She set it in front of Karyn and added a glass of orange juice. "Yum. Vaughn would be so jealous."

Dori brought her mug and took a seat, too. "I really appreciate your help. I shop online a lot, living in the boonies as I do, but not for clothes. Especially not for vacation clothes. But finding the right outfits in December for a tropical vacation would be impossible at the mall. I almost decided to go without a suitcase and buy what I need there."

"You could certainly do that. You'd pay a fortune

over there, however. Even with overnight shipping, I bet I can save you fifty percent. And if anything needs altering, I can do that, too—if you or someone has a sewing machine."

"I do. I'm forever patching things."

"Oh, man, this is so delicious, Dori. Can you show me how to cook potatoes like this? I always seem to burn mine, especially if I add onions."

"The trick is to cook the potatoes on medium until they're golden and crispy, then add caramelized onions you made ahead of time just long enough to warm them. Sometimes people are in too much of a hurry and use too high a temperature. Do you like to cook?"

"I cook to live. I eat out too much. Aside from all the cooking, what else do you do?"

"I grow most of the vegetables we eat, although now that we have Annie, I get a lot from her. She grows all year, and I've been a fair-weather gardener myself. I'm bookkeeper and buyer, and I help on the ranch when I'm needed. Jill-of-all-trades. My first aid skills are occasionally called upon for animals *and* people."

"Raising six children must've taken all your time."

"And was an utter joy. Honestly, I would've had a couple more if my body hadn't decided otherwise. I'd love it if my children would all get busy having children of their own. It'll be fun having a baby around again this summer. Mitch was born to be a father. He's always been great with kids."

"And Vaughn?"

"He surprised me. He'd never been one to talk about

being a father, but he took to it right away. He's done a good job of raising Cass."

"I can see that." Karyn bit into a piece of bacon and closed her eyes. "You can't find bacon like this in a grocery store."

Dori smiled. "We trade beef for pork with a friend. We both admit we're spoiled." She wrapped her hands around her mug. "Are you enjoying your stay?"

"Very much. It's not an easy life, though, is it?"

"It has plenty of rewards." She lightly touched Karyn's arm. "You realize I have a lot of questions about you, and I would be asking them so that I could know you better, but I don't think my son would appreciate it. He did tell me about your brother. I was so sorry to hear that."

"Did he tell you we were twins?"

"No."

"Kyle and I were extraordinarily close, as you can imagine." She crumpled up her napkin, then carried her plate to the sink to rinse. "If you wouldn't mind showing me your closet, I can get a better idea of what you like."

"I'd like to wear boots like yours, but I'm sure I'd fall over."

"In *Hawaii?*"

Dori laughed. "No. In general."

"Oh. Well, would you like to try mine on? We look like we wear the same size. These have a shorter heel than most of my others."

"Would I? Yes!"

Karyn loved watching Dori walk across the big master bedroom and back as if she were a model, giggling all the way. After, they settled at the computer. Using her contacts, Karyn chose vacation garments that would also work at home—for the most part. A bathing suit and cover-up wouldn't get much use after the trip, but the two silky nightgowns would. They ordered a few things for Jim, too, as a surprise.

After almost two hours, they were done. "Everything should arrive tomorrow," Karyn said, satisfied.

"That was fun," Dori said, slouching, then rolling her shoulders. "But harder work than mucking the stable. And you do this every day?"

"I generally shop in person. I've built up relationships with a lot of retailers who treat me very well. I try to keep my business local."

"What's it like, being around movie stars?"

"It can be fun. And exciting sometimes, too. Every day is different."

"How'd you end up in Hollywood?"

"Kyle decided to go to college out here, and I followed. I worked for a personal shopper for a few years, then she quit and I was able to keep her clients."

"Well, you have a very good eye. I think I'm going to love everything."

"I'm glad. We can return anything you don't want." Karyn glanced at the office clock. "I need to get going. I've got some photographs to take before the sun gets too high."

Jim was coming through the door as Karyn left.

"Am I going to find a happy wife now?"

"I believe you will."

"Bless you."

Karyn laughed. "My pleasure."

She drove around the countryside for an hour, finding it easy to get her bearings because of the stunning snowcapped Gold Ridge Mountain visible from every vantage point. According to Cassidy, Bigfoot lived there. She wondered if he was hibernating now.

Even in the winter, the landscape was gorgeous—harsh and barren on the surface but craggy with leafless trees that painted pictures against the sky.

She found several places she'd like to paint and marked their locations on the map, itching to start. She was excited about it, something she hadn't felt in a long time.

Every so often she checked her cell phone, hoping for a connection to check her messages. She finally got two bars. She had seven messages from clients wanting her to do some returns of gifts, one from her mother checking to see how she was feeling and one from Gloriana: "Just checking on you, Karyn. I hope you survived Christmas okay. Give me a call when you can."

She returned calls to say she was on vacation, called her parents and left a message on their answering machine, then headed back to the ranch house. It'd been a good day, with a lot of hours still left. She would get Cassidy to sit for a while today so that it looked like she was accomplishing something. Every free moment she had she'd been sketching, improving at the skill.

As she pulled into Vaughn's front yard, Karyn wondered if they would have time for another make-out session before Cass got home. Anticipation rose in her at the thought, but when she opened the front door he was standing there, waiting for her, his expression grim.

"There's been a hitch," he said.

Chapter Nine

"The test results are back?" Karyn asked, her face paling, her voice catching.

"No, although there's a hitch there, too. I called the lab this morning to see when we could expect the results. They've got a backlog because they're awaiting a replacement part for a piece of broken equipment and they have low staffing during the holidays. They'll get to it as soon as they can, they said." Vaughn wouldn't have been annoyed about that because he wasn't in a hurry to have Karyn leave, but now, after the message he'd received, it was a different story. He wanted to know *now.* "Let's sit down."

"This must be really bad news," she said as they took seats in the living room.

Vaughn leaned toward her, resting his arms on his

thighs. "This morning I talked to a man Ginger dated years ago. He'd been trying to find her. He reached her ex-roommate, the one who gave me Kyle's name, and she told him I was looking for anyone she'd gone out with seven years ago. His name is Jason Humphreys. He lives in Seattle now."

"And he thinks he could be the father?"

"Definitely could be, given the timeline."

"Ginger was a busy woman."

"That's putting it nicely." It proved how little he'd known her. He would never marry again without knowing someone at least a year.

"So, now what?"

"We decided to wait on your DNA results before he bothered being tested."

"You said he was looking for Ginger. Did he tell you why?"

"He didn't volunteer the information, and I didn't ask."

"Was he the only other name you had as a possibility?"

"No." There'd been a couple others, but he'd been able to eliminate them. He felt like such a fool for falling for Ginger, believing her story about the father abandoning her, offering only to pay for an abortion. Would he ever find out the truth?

"How was your day?" he asked Karyn, needing to change the subject.

It took her a few seconds to shift gears. "Um, I had a lot of fun with your mom. Your dad's going to be very surprised at a couple of her purchases." She wiggled her eyebrows.

He winced. "Too much information, Hollywood."

She took great delight in his discomfort. "Think red and cut down to here—" She dragged her fingers down her chest to a spot between her breasts.

"I'm going to superimpose an image of you wearing something like that. No way I want to picture my mother." He moved to sit next to her on the couch. "Do you own something similar?"

"Not that I brought with me."

His pulse thudded. "Red?"

She nodded.

"See-through?"

"In places." Her smile was mysterious.

"When's the last time you wore it?"

She jabbed his arm. "Which is a sneaky way of asking me about my sexual past. If we reach that point in our relationship, I'll volunteer the info, as I would expect you to also." She laid her hands on his chest. "I believe the agreement we have for now is to make out a lot."

He took that as an invitation, drawing her over him to straddle his lap. She leaned down, their lips brushed—

"So what qualifies as making out?" he asked against her mouth. "First base? Second? Third?" He slid his hands under her stretchy white top, resting them along her rib cage.

"We've already gotten to second. If third includes

me getting to touch you, too, I'm game." She rocked against him a little.

He drew a quick, hard breath, then cupped her breasts, her silky bra not a barrier for her hard nipples as he brushed them with his thumbs. "Something tells me it's not going to be easy to stick to the plan," he muttered.

"We can amend the contract as needed."

"I do like that you're flexible."

She ended the conversation with her lips and tongue and teeth, tugging on his lower lip, sweeping his mouth with her tongue, pressing her hips to his. He let her take the lead—for the moment. Then he discovered the front clasp of her bra and flicked it open. Her breasts spilled into his hands, her warm flesh feeling like heaven. Her body was soft in all the right places and smelled faintly of vanilla. When he shoved up her top, she straightened, giving him free access to look at her, to taste her, to suck her puckered nipples into his mouth, using his teeth and tongue on her until she was moaning....

Karyn hooked her fingers into his jeans, holding on as he lavished attention on her breasts. She inched her hands closer together until she touched his own hot, hard flesh. His hips rose suddenly, violently. He groaned, a flattering, arousing sound.

He grabbed her hair and kissed her thoroughly, delightfully, taking charge. She loved how he could be so civilized most of the time, then such an alpha male when things turned intimate. She imagined him in bed, devouring her, delighting—

"Daddy! Come in, Daddy! This is Cassidy. Over."

They jerked apart. Karyn looked around frantically.

"Walkie-talkie," he said, helping her off his lap and then grabbing the device from the table by the front door. "Come in, Cass. Over."

"Uncle Mitch says to tell you we'll be home soon. I wanted to surprise you, but he said it probably wasn't a good idea." There was a pause. "Oh, yeah, over."

He glanced at Karyn, his brows raised. "Did you have fun? Over."

"Actually, it was kinda boring. Over."

Vaughn smiled. Karyn figured he wouldn't have to worry about his daughter wanting to repeat the experience anytime in the near future.

Karyn found her bra clasp and was about to hook it, but Vaughn shook his head. "Allow me," he mouthed.

"How's Belle? Over."

"She's resting up so that she can play with you when you get back. Over."

"Fifteen minutes, Uncle Mitch says. Over."

"See you then, sweetheart. Over and out."

"Over and out, Daddy."

"Good ol' Uncle Mitch," Vaughn said, moving toward Karyn like a wolf stalking its prey. "I guess we haven't hidden our attraction at all. Even my father noticed."

She frowned. "Well, crap."

He lifted her top and found her bra clasp. "I had a good time, Hollywood. Did you?"

"Rhetorical question, Lawman."

He grinned at her new nickname. "That makes me feel like I should be packin' six-shooters."

"You are. One, anyway."

He kissed her, a soft merging of mouths and breath. "I'd like to challenge you to a duel sometime."

"I just might accept. But for now I'd like to go make myself presentable before we have company."

Karyn hurried upstairs. It wasn't until she was spritzing water on her hair to restore her curls that she realized she hadn't thought about the news Vaughn had given her. She also realized exactly how much she'd been counting on Cassidy being Kyle's.

So much was at stake, and she had no control over any of it.

Except for her relationship with Vaughn. Although she couldn't say she'd exerted control there. In fact, she might have given up all control to him if Cassidy hadn't called his name.

He could talk anyone into anything, his mother had said. Actually, he didn't even have to use words, Karyn thought, although she couldn't share that with his mother.

And Karyn was starting to like his family too much.

How much more complicated could it get?

She reached the bottom of the staircase as Cassidy raced in and leaped into her arms.

"I'm home!"

"You certainly are." She held on to the girl for a few seconds then set her down, thrilled at the easy gesture. "Was it fun?"

"It was very cold. Hi, Daddy!" He kneeled, holding a leashed Belle. Cassidy looked like she couldn't decide who to hug first. Belle won, wriggling her way free of Vaughn.

"Can I take a hot bath, Daddy?"

"You sure can. Right after you groom and feed My Little."

"Uncle Brody said he'd do it."

Karen laughed as Cassidy fluttered her lashes at her father.

"You know the rules. Your horse, your job. I'll help."

She scuffed her way out of the house. Vaughn smiled and shook his head at Karyn. "Want to come and observe?"

"Sure. I'll grab my jacket."

"Meet you outside. I want to thank my brothers."

By the time Karyn caught up with them in the barn, My Little had been unsaddled and Cassidy was giving her food and water. Karyn leaned against a stall door to watch.

"Okay, walk her around the paddock a few times," Vaughn said. "Slow and easy, Cass."

"Okay."

"It takes a lot to care for a horse, doesn't it?" Karyn asked as she and Vaughn followed. "Cassidy hardly seems old enough for the task."

"She's given more responsibility every year. Not only is she learning how important it is to care for her horse, but she's learning patience, too. Cooling down a horse takes a great deal of patience. You have to judge how hot they are and when they've actually cooled down enough. It takes time and practice."

They draped their arms over the paddock fence. "I take it that big ol' intimidating-looking black horse in the other stall is yours."

"You think Satan is intimidating?"

"Satan?" She looked toward the barn nervously. "Should Cass be near him?"

Vaughn angled toward her a little. "Actually, his name is Gatsby, the Great Gatsby, in fact, and he's the least intimidating horse I know."

"He's monstrously large."

"I guess he might seem so, if you have nothing to compare him with. If you're interested in riding, there are several well-trained mounts at the homestead you could choose from."

"I understand that horses can sense someone's fear."

"True."

"Then I'll pass, thanks."

A beat passed. "Suit yourself."

She thought he looked disappointed.

He stepped down from the rail and looked as if he was going to walk away. She put a hand on his arm, stopping him.

"Is it important to you that I ride?"

"It's a great way to see the ranch, especially since you're scouting places to paint."

"You didn't answer my question, Lawman."

Vaughn rested a shoulder against the rail. He couldn't tell her the truth, that Ginger had never ridden and that he'd resented her for it, as if what he did, where he lived, didn't matter. He tried not to compare Karyn to Ginger, but comparisons kept popping up.

However, at the moment Karyn was just looking for an honest answer. "I would enjoy showing you why I love it here so much that I changed my entire life to come back."

"Then I'll give it a shot. You must be a sight to behold, wearing all black and riding a black stallion."

"Gelding. And I have an image to maintain." He grinned lazily.

"You like to be in charge. You like power."

He shrugged. "If people perceive that about me, I rarely have to exert power to get what I want."

"I find it a turn-on, myself," she said. "Not that I want you to overpower me but that you don't let anyone overpower *you*. That kind of self-confidence is sexy."

He found her take fascinating. "Hollywood, you are self-confidently sexy yourself."

"It's the shoes."

He laughed. Although if he were being honest, he would admit that her shoes probably were a small part of his attraction to her, mostly for what they accentuated—her legs and rear. And her very sexy walk, which often made him stop in his tracks to watch.

"Am I done yet?" Cassidy said as she approached.

"Let's see how sweaty she is." He went into the paddock and ran a hand down her flanks. "Okay. Let's go rub her down."

"I'm going to get my camera," Karyn said. "Cass, I

sure would like to have you sit for a little while today. Are you up to it?"

Vaughn made eye contact with his daughter, signaling what her answer should be.

"After I play with Belle, please. She missed me."

"Of course." Karyn headed toward the house. She was wearing what she called her work boots, with the three-inch heels, and he was mesmerized by her. Her rear end was the finest he'd ever seen, firm and round and high. He wanted to get her naked and nibble on—

"Daddy!"

He dragged his gaze away. "What?"

"I said I really like Karyn."

Which worried him a little, but he said, "Me, too." They walked side by side to the barn.

"I want sparkly shoes like hers."

Karyn had already warned him about that. "As long as they're flats."

She cheered. "And I wanna get my ears pierced."

He supposed next she would ask for a tattoo.... Which made him wonder if Karyn had any. "When you're ten."

"Ten? That's so old! All my friends have their ears pierced."

"I'll tell you what. I'll take you to school one day, and if all the other girls in your class have pierced ears, you can, too."

She looked away. "I didn't say that. I said all my *friends*."

He fought a smile. She was way too smart. "You

make a list of your friends, and I'll think about it. All your friends, Cass. Not just the ones with pierced ears."

He could tell by her expression that she'd fudged her facts a little. He was looking forward to seeing how she handled it.

"Can we go shopping tomorrow? To the mall?"

"In Medford? Sure." He hadn't planned on working anyway.

"Can I choose a new outfit to wear for my portrait?"

"You got a lot of new outfits for Christmas."

"I want something like Karyn wears. You know, something frilly."

And so it begins, Vaughn thought. She seemed to have forgotten she would be wearing ranch clothes. His little tomboy was growing up.

Way too fast.

Chapter Ten

The next day, they dropped off Belle with Dori and Jim and drove to Medford to the big mall. Vaughn had never been more bored in his life.

"It's too grown up for you, Cass," Karyn said when Cassidy held up a dark blue blouse with a ruffle along a low scoop neck.

"But this is the girls' section, and I'm a girl."

"It's not right. Plus the color's wrong for you." She pulled another top from the rack. "This pink would be perfect."

"Ooh. That's pretty." She reached for it. "I do kinda like that, especially the lacy stuff."

"Let's try it on." Karyn gave Vaughn a be-patient-a-little-longer smile.

He couldn't remember seeing Cass in pink, not since she'd started choosing her own clothes. He wandered away, although he kept the dressing room door in view because he knew his opinion would be sought.

His cell phone rang. His mother. "Is everything okay?" He had visions of Belle chewing on his parents' sofa.

"Fine. I wanted to ask a favor of Karyn, but I don't have her number."

"Hold on a sec. She and Cass are in the dressing room." He walked in that direction.

"While I've got you, son, I was wondering if you all would like to come to dinner?"

"I don't see why not."

"Also, my vacation clothes arrived, and I'd like Karyn to take a look."

They came through the doorway. Cass had a big smile on her face. The pink fabric put color in her cheeks. Vaughn could tell she was pleased with how she looked.

"Mom wants to talk to you," Vaughn said to Karyn, passing her the phone. "You look very pretty, sweetheart."

Cassidy twirled. "Thank you."

A few seconds later, Karyn handed the phone back to him. "Girl stuff," she said with a wink.

Vaughn didn't want to know.

"I wonder if there's an art supply store here. Maybe I should pick up supplies, in case… Well, it would look good anyway. I'd need an easel and palette and a ton of paints. Brushes. Everything."

"We'll check it out."

"And maybe after Cass changes," Karyn said, "you and she could get an ice cream or something while I take care of something for your mom."

"I don't think I'll have a hard time convincing Cass of that."

After Karyn walked away, Vaughn decided he was curious about the call after all. He also realized his mother never would've asked Ginger for a favor. For years his mother had tried to connect with her daughter-in-law, but Ginger had never warmed up to her, although his mother had never said a word against her. Not once.

A while later Vaughn spotted Karyn from a couple hundred feet away strolling down the middle of the mall walkway, her head up, a slight smile on her face, her zebra-striped bag swinging. She didn't teeter, not the tiniest bit, yet she was wearing heels of at least five inches.

Other men paid attention, some directly, some more covertly. She was a presence.

Until he'd met her, he wouldn't have ranked curly hair as something sexy. Cass's hair was curly. It was cute. But on Karyn—

"Do you think Karyn is sexy, Daddy?"

He almost spit out his water. In an effort to keep communication open, however, he said, "What do you think that means?"

"It's when men look at a girl kinda funny. Like you were doing. Your eyes got squinty."

Out of the mouths of babes. "Well, that's not what it means, not exactly, and it's a word I don't think you're ready to use."

"What *does* it mean?"

Karyn came up beside them. "Do I have time to get myself an ice cream?"

He stood, relieved not to answer Cass's question. Yet. She would come back to it sometime. "I'll get it. What would you like?"

"I can do it, but thank you. Oh, no art supply store here, by the way. Maybe I'll order them online." She gave him a great view from behind as she walked away again.

Because Cass was again studying him, he didn't stare.

"I wonder what she bought," Cassidy said. "She doesn't have a shopping bag."

She brought back a single-dip ice cream cone, which meant he would have to sit there and watch her lick and swirl it, imagining her—

"What did you get?" Cass asked her.

"Mocha almond fudge."

Cass giggled. "I mean, what did you buy?"

"Something for your grammie." Karyn patted her purse. "I can't tell you. It's a secret. Don't frown. I've got something for you, too. For when we get home."

"Can you hurry, please?"

"Cass."

Vaughn's no-nonsense tone had Cassidy sitting back in her chair and swinging her feet. She pretended to zip her lips with her fingers. Karyn saw that even Vaughn had trouble not laughing. She was definitely a little character.

A tired one, too. She fell asleep before they got on the freeway to head back to the ranch, about an hour's drive. Karyn yawned, crossed her arms and settled into her seat.

"Sleep if you want," Vaughn said. "It's been a busy day, with more to come."

"Maybe." They weren't really free to talk because Cass was in the backseat and kids were good at pretending to sleep. "What'd you like best about growing up here?"

"The freedom. We all had a lot of responsibilities, but we weren't supervised once we'd mastered something, so it felt like we were independent in a way. Even so, I couldn't wait to leave home and go to college and law school."

"You were a good student."

"I loved school. Loved learning. All six of us have college degrees. Mom and Dad were insistent on that, not just for the education but for learning how to live on our own, figuring out how to get through life. They paid for half, and we had to figure out the rest. How about you?"

"I'm more of a commonsense person. I tried college for a while, but I didn't have a plan, therefore no major, therefore it made no sense to me to keep going.

My parents are both professors at a small college in Vermont, and they were disappointed. In a way I regret not sticking with it for the very reasons you were made to go. Every once in a while I think about going back to school."

"What would you major in this time around?"

"Guess."

"Art."

She nodded. "I'd be a good student now. I can't believe how much my drawing skills have improved in just the few days I've been here. I hadn't taken the time to practice in a long time." She yawned again.

"Rest your eyes, Hollywood." He patted her thigh but didn't let his hand linger.

The next thing she knew, they were parking in front of the homestead.

"Can I have my surprise now?" Cass asked sleepily, not even fully awake yet.

Karyn and Vaughn looked at each other and laughed. "When we get in the house," Karyn said, enjoying the little girl more every minute.

All of the Ryder clan were there for dinner. Even Haley drove out from town. Hugs were exchanged. Karyn felt out of place in her "city clothes."

"Your blouse is gorgeous," Jenny said, fingering the lace on the collar. "I could never pull this off. I'm way too country."

"So do you plan to come back here when you're done with college?"

"Here, but not *here*. Shh. I haven't told my parents my plans yet."

Cassidy tugged on Karyn's hand. "Now, please."

They hurried hand in hand down the hall to Vaughn's old bedroom. Karyn pulled out a small bag and passed it to Cass. Inside it were three headbands, including one that was just a row of rhinestones.

"Oooh. A crown."

Karyn didn't know how Vaughn felt about the whole princess phenomenon. She probably should have asked him before giving her the rhinestone one.

"They're all headbands," she said. "This is your dress-up one, and the others are for casual wear. It'll keep your hair out of your eyes. Do you want to wear one?"

"Yes, please. The crown."

She waited for Cass to make eye contact. "It's not a crown. It's a headband. Okay?"

Cassidy nodded, but Karyn wasn't sure she'd made her point. She might end up in an uncomfortable conversation with Vaughn later.

She showed Cass how to put it on and fix her hair around it.

"Can I wear my pink blouse?"

"I think this works fine."

"I have to go show my daddy." Off she went, Karyn trailing a little more slowly behind her.

It only took one look at Vaughn to know she'd made a mistake. And now they had to get through an entire evening with his family before she could deal with it.

But first Dori pulled Karyn away, much like Cass had.

"Did you find it?" Dori asked, excitement in her voice and expression.

Karyn dug into her purse for another bag. "He can never know I shopped for this. I could never look him in the eye."

Dori held up a pair of red silk boxers. "Perfect. I can't wait to see his face when I ask him to wear them." She almost folded in half from laughing. "We'll make quite a pair in our matching reds."

"Indeed you will. Now tell me, did everything you ordered arrive today?"

"Everything. If you could come by in the morning, I'll try it all on and see what we think."

"I'd be happy to. Were the turquoise sandals as cute as they looked online?"

"They're perfect. I also made an appointment for a pedicure, my first ever. Usually my toes don't show."

"Coral would work with all your outfits."

"Okay." She grabbed Karyn's arm and leaned close. "Jim has no idea what he started by giving me that trip. I feel like I'm about to go on my honeymoon again. Except this time I'll know what I'm doing! Thank you so much."

They didn't stay too late. Dinner was casual—grilled steaks, fries and a baby greens salad from Annie's garden—with plenty of conversation, although not between Vaughn and Karyn. Cass kept running into the bathroom to admire her "crown," which didn't help.

Back at Vaughn's house, Karyn told Cassidy good-night at the bottom of the stairs, then waited in the living room for him to come back down. This was one of those times when she should've asked for permission first instead of apologizing later.

She sat cross-legged on the floor, letting Belle crawl all over her. Vaughn was probably reading Cass a story—or letting her read one to him, which took longer. It seemed to be a regular bedtime ritual.

Belle had settled down in Karyn's lap when Vaughn came down the stairs slowly, each step pounding a death knell. She didn't shirk, nor did she show false courage.

"You've been here for five days," he said. "In that time my daughter has changed from being comfortable in jeans and a T-shirt to one who wants lacy blouses and crowns."

"I told her it was a headband, not a crown. Truly. I meant no harm. I was trying to figure out things she could do with her hair herself. I should've asked you first."

"She's not yours, Karyn."

He didn't say it unkindly but with a certain amount of sympathy. That didn't mean he would forgive her.

"I know."

He crouched down. "Do you? Ever since you got here you've been cozy with her. What if, Karyn? What if? It's one thing for me to get hurt. I can deal with it the way I have in the past. But not Cass. She deserves her childhood."

He thinks I could hurt him? "I won't buy her anything else. I'll try to limit my time with her, if that's what you want. Or maybe I should go to the motel, after all, and wait there." Tears pushed at her eyes. She tried to keep them from falling. "I'm not staking a claim on Cassidy. People can't just be nice? Especially to a child?"

Vaughn pushed himself up and went to the fireplace. He'd readied it before they'd gone to Medford, so he only needed to light it, but he hesitated. Damn her. How could he criticize her after that speech? And he had more to say, but he knew it had more to do with trying to keep his distance from her himself. He could feel himself getting too involved, but he was determined not to repeat his mistakes.

"What happens if this Jason Humphreys turns out to be her father?" Vaughn said. "Her world is going to turn upside down. For her to lose you when she's gotten so close, so fast, might be too much. And don't tell me kids are resilient. Every child is different, and her mother already abandoned her. She deals with that every day."

Karyn stood, bringing Belle with her and placing her in Vaughn's hands. She crossed her arms. "You're protecting your daughter. I get that. You're a great dad. So I'll leave in the morning. I'll tell her I got an emergency call and had to go home."

He didn't watch her walk away, but he knew the route she traveled—across the living room, then the foyer, then up the staircase. She hadn't accused him of anything—oh, say, for example, being too possessive of his daughter and too worried about getting hurt himself. About how he should be starting to live again, not spending most of his days on the ranch, where he was safe from emotional crises.

He stared at the floor.

Muttering a few creative curse words, he set down the dog, climbed the staircase, then walked directly to Karyn's room. He knocked quietly. After a few seconds she opened the door.

"I'm sorry," he said. Apologizing was something he rarely did because he usually thought things through first. "I was taking out my frustration about Jason—and Ginger, too, I suppose—on you."

"It's okay."

"I'm sorry I made you cry." Because he could see she had, in fact, been crying since she'd left the living room. She looked more fragile than he'd seen her.

"Thank you."

"Don't go, Karyn. I don't want you to leave, and I know Cass would second that."

"Okay." She whispered the word.

Then he realized why she seemed not as strong as usual. She had her shoes off, which took inches off her height. It made him even more protective. He took a mental step back.

"Can I get you something? Hot tea? Cocoa? Brandy?"

She shook her head, but he didn't want to leave.

"Why don't you get ready for bed and I'll bring you hot chocolate?"

"You don't have to take care of me, Vaughn."

Was that what he was doing? "It's just a cup of cocoa."

"Fine. Okay."

"Is ten minutes long enough?"

"Yes."

Vaughn timed warming the drink so that it would keep its heat. He put Belle in her crate in his room, and she let him know how unhappy she was. But there could be only one alpha dog in the house.

She'd left her door open a crack and the bathroom light on, but that door was mostly closed, too. He could see she was sitting up in bed.

"You do realize it's only nine o'clock?" she said, accepting the mug. "I never go to bed this early."

"You've got a TV." He picked up the remote and handed it to her. "Or you could finish your drink, and I'll stay with you until you fall asleep."

She smiled at last. "Will you read me a bedtime story?"

Belle howled.

"Go, Dog. Go?" Vaughn asked. He found her feet through the blanket and rubbed them as she drank. Sounds of pleasure escaped her. He pushed the blanket aside from her knees down, changed his position a little and drew her feet into his lap.

"You don't have to make anything up to me, Vaughn. I was the one who was wrong."

"I could've handled it differently. You seem so strong most of the time that I forget how hard this all must be for you."

"I wouldn't trade the time with you and Cassidy for anything." She set her mug aside and closed her eyes.

He got up and turned off the bathroom light, then returned to her. He liked the dark, liked the possibilities that night brought when you couldn't see everything clearly, making you feel your way through instead. Her feet were smooth and delicate. He pressed his thumbs into her arches and got a response. He wondered if she made the same noises during sex.

"We haven't made out in bed," she said, her voice soft and a little sleepy sounding.

"There's probably a good reason for that." He could only restrain himself so much for so long.

"We could set a time limit. Five minutes, then we quit."

"Dreamer."

"You don't think we could quit?" she asked, rising up on her elbows.

"I'm no masochist." He tucked her feet back under the covers. "I take it you're not ready to sleep."

"Not yet."

"Tell you what. I'll take Belle out and change into something more comfortable, then I'll come back and we'll talk about it some more."

"You are the talkiest man I've ever known. Don't you do anything spur of the moment?"

"That's how mistakes happen. See you in a bit."

"Maybe," she said in a self-affronted tone that made him smile.

Needing to cool down his desires, he took his time walking the dog, who was not nearly as uncontrollable as she'd been at the beginning. Then he crated her, changed into pajama bottoms and a T-shirt, the same as Karyn, and headed back to her room. He crept inside, hoping she was asleep—and hoping she was awake. As he neared the bed, she folded back the covers in welcome.

He climbed in. She immediately slid close to him. He wrapped an arm around her as she rested hers on his chest, a leg atop his, and sighed, her breath a warm rush against him. Her vanilla scent tickled his nose. He was already hard with need. He'd purposely not brought a condom with him. Losing control was not an option.

But she was hell-bent on making out, so he could tantalize her, make her lose control instead.

"If you take off your T-shirt," he said, "and stretch out on top of me, I'll give you a backrub."

She sat up and peeled off her shirt. There was just enough light from the moon outside her window to see her tempting breasts. He wouldn't touch them, he decided, would leave her wanting more. Just a backrub.

"You take your shirt off, too," she said.

He whipped his over his head, then helped her settle on top of him, her breasts pressed against his chest, skin to skin.

"So, you even pack your six-shooter in bed, Lawman. That's risky."

He smiled, then began to massage her back, her skin silken, the ridges of her spine fascinating. He followed that trail all the way down to the tip of her tailbone, then cupped her rear and massaged her there, too.

Karyn couldn't hold still. His hands felt wonderful as they squeezed then soothed. His erection flattered her. She wanted to throw back the covers, get naked and take him inside her. She'd been foolish to believe she could lie with him so intimately and not want a conclusion.

"You're giving off a lot of heat," he said close to her ear.

"What a surprise."

His chest shook with laughter.

"You have incredible hands," she said. "Talented."

"The better to feel your incredible body, my dear."

"I'd like to do the same to you." She gasped as his fingers met in the middle of her rear and stroked her temptingly.

"Not this time, Hollywood."

"You have way too much self-control."

"You have way too little." Rolling them both to their sides, he tugged at her pajama bottoms.

She not only let him, she helped him, until she was blessedly naked. He shoved the blankets down at the same time. Exposed, she waited for an onslaught of attention, but he surprised her as his fingertips barely grazed her, leaving trails of goose bumps across her body. Her nipples ached for his mouth, but he only used his fingers, circling them, then sliding down her abdomen and beyond. She arched up.

"You're so hot," he whispered, pressing the heel of his hand against her, sliding a finger inside.

She struggled to breathe. He didn't let up until she was done, blocking the sounds she made with his mouth in a deep, searching kiss. She didn't come down all the way but wanted more.

Wanted *him,* not just the feeling.

"I want to do the same for you," she said.

"I'm all right." But his body belied his words. She could bounce coins off him, he was so taut.

"That's not fair."

"I'm okay with that," he said.

"I meant you're denying me, not just yourself. I want to please you, to know that I have."

He was quiet a long time, then he said, "Hands only. It won't take long. I've been in a state since I watched you eat your ice cream."

She liked that he was direct with her, not making her guess what he wanted or liked. She liked that he let loose in bed, that he'd obviously made a study of lovemaking.

She wasn't as experienced. She wanted to take time getting to know specifically what he liked, but she barely got her hands on him before he was true to his own words.

After a little while, he pulled his clothes on and climbed out of bed. "Sleep well," he said.

"Almost home base," she said in return.

"Enough to provide some damn good fantasies."

Her room felt empty after he left. *She* felt empty. She wasn't a modern woman, after all. She couldn't have sex for the pure physical enjoyment of it, but needed the emotional involvement, too.

She was falling in love with him, which was a really stupid thing to do. They came from two different worlds. She may have a blood relationship with his daughter, but who knew how that would turn out? She lived and worked in Hollywood. His place was here. He had no desire to move away from his life on the ranch.

Should she let herself fall in love with him or fight it?

Karyn pulled the blankets over her and closed her eyes. So much to think about. So many decisions to make.

And a new fantasy to enjoy in the meantime.

Chapter Eleven

The next morning, after the frost melted, they all headed to the homestead. Karyn drove over first, taking Belle with her. Vaughn and Cassidy would follow on horseback.

She'd slept for eight solid hours and woke up dreaming about Vaughn, almost expecting him to be beside her in bed. She felt a little shy around him at breakfast, and he was quiet, too, but gave her such heated looks she thought she might spontaneously combust.

Jim was out riding fence, so Karyn and Dori had the house to themselves for a while. Belle gnawed on a rawhide bone as Dori tried on various outfits. One needed to be returned, but otherwise everything fit perfectly. Karyn convinced her to wear sandals, cropped pants and a tropical blouse on the plane. Their flight was at 6:30 a.m., but Jenny would be dropping them off, so they only had to make their way from the car to the terminal entrance in the cold weather.

"I'm not sure we'll get Jim to agree to leave his Wranglers and boots behind," Dori said. "We plan on visiting a friend's cattle ranch while we're there."

"Has he seen his new clothes yet?"

"I'm going to spring them on him tomorrow when I pack. They're nothing like he usually wears."

"Tell him he'll stick out like a sore thumb if he dresses for home."

"Getting him to leave his hat behind will probably be the hardest part. He'll feel naked without it."

"And hot with it, but it's not worth arguing about, I think. I'm sure you'll figure out how to convince him— or not. It's only important that you relax and have fun."

"I'll remind him, thank you. How much longer are you staying, Karyn?"

"No clue."

"You have a job to get back to, I imagine."

"I told my clients I would be gone for two weeks. Some don't believe me because I never take longer than a week. It helps that I don't have cell reception. If they're calling, I never know until I go somewhere within range of a tower." From the bedroom window Karyn saw Vaughn and Cass approach. "He makes quite a statement on that horse."

"All my sons are strong men, but Vaughn has something extra," Dori said, coming up next to Karyn. "I got to watch him in a courtroom a few times. I hadn't seen that side of him. He was fascinating. I burst my buttons. He has depths I hadn't seen and intelligence beyond the norm, which I *had* seen. He's a financial genius and negotiates great contracts for us. I'm only sorry that he's had a tough time personally. Ginger really played him."

Dori clamped her mouth shut, as if realizing she'd said too much.

"He's talked about her," Karyn said. "You didn't say anything I didn't already know."

"I'm generally good at keeping my children's private lives private. I don't know why I worry about him more than the rest, even the girls."

It took a while longer until Vaughn and Cass came into the house.

"Did we give you enough time?" he asked, giving his mother a hug.

"Plenty."

"You're done?" he asked Karyn.

"Your mom is going to turn more heads than usual. Especially your father's."

"Good. We just saddled a horse for you."

Panic set in like a gut punch, quick and breath stealing. "I haven't shopped for the right clothes yet. No riding boots." She lifted a leg, showing off her inappropriate footwear.

"We already know we wear the same size," Dori said. "You can borrow mine. Your clothes are fine. I can give you a warmer jacket."

"Traitor," Karyn said.

"You told me you were ready to try," Vaughn said. "No time like the present. It's a beautiful day. We'll take it slow and easy."

"I'll pack you a lunch."

"Thanks, Mom."

Everyone looked at Karyn expectantly. She wished she was pregnant like Annie so she'd have an excuse....

The thought hung there. Pregnant. She'd never really thought about it before, except in a when-I-have-children-someday kind of way. She glanced at Vaughn. She already knew what kind of father he was. There would be no guessing about that.

"Karyn?" the man filling her thoughts said.

"Hmm? What?"

"Mom's brought boots and a jacket."

"And a hat and gloves."

Before she knew it, she was standing next to a beautiful horse named Beauty, who had a white blaze down her nose. She belonged to his sister Haley, who didn't get to ride often, so everyone took turns keeping her exercised.

Karyn's heart pounded like crazy as Vaughn showed her how to mount up, then gave her basic lessons on using the reins. Beauty barely budged when Karyn got aboard, not shifting her legs at all.

"She's very well trained," Vaughn said. "You won't have to guide her much. She'll follow us."

The animal felt so big and so strong under her. Karyn made eye contact with Vaughn as he mounted Gatsby.

"She wouldn't even flinch at a rattler," he said, his voice soothing. "Not that there are any this time of year," he added in a hurry when she panicked.

Cassidy seemed to be enjoying it all. Her grin never diminished. And she looked adorable with her hair in pigtails poking out from under her red hat.

"Ready?" Vaughn asked.

She glanced at Dori. "I haven't written a will."

"Tell the lawyer your wishes as you ride."

"Enough stalling, Hollywood. Give her a squeeze with your boots. Let's go. Slow walk at first."

Karyn didn't know what she'd expected but it wasn't this…this excitement. At first she thought it was fear, but soon she realized she was also having fun. She'd been born knowing how to do this or something. It was innate. Yet she'd never sat on a horse before.

"You're doing great," Vaughn said.

"I know!" She laughed. "Even though I'm scared to death!"

A slow grin came over his face. "Want to kick it up a notch? I know Cass would."

"Lead the way."

"Cass, get out ahead of us and go into a trot. We'll follow you."

"Oh, boy!"

"Keep your back straight and body relaxed, like I told you," he said to Karyn. "You'll bounce but in the right way. I'll be right beside you."

He talked to her constantly, correcting and advising. At first the pace had her catching her breath, then she got into the rhythm of it. Cold air chilled her face, making her smile a little stiff. She flashed as much of a grin at Vaughn as she could manage with her cheeks frozen.

"I love this!" she shouted, the adrenaline rush huge.

"I can see that."

They rode until they reached what appeared to be a small graveyard. A bench had been built to one side, and it sat in the sun now as they ate their lunch and let the horses rest. Then Karyn wandered through the headstones, finding Ryder family members who'd been born as far back as the early 1800s. She stopped in front of the one who'd died most recently, George Hiram Ryder, who'd passed away just over three years ago.

"My father's father," Vaughn said, kneeling to clear some dead leaves.

"He always had butterscotch candies in his pockets," Cass said.

"The strong, silent type, unless he was correcting your mistakes," Vaughn said, smiling. "He and Mitch were inseparable. Mitch took his death really hard. There's a family history written out at the homestead, if you're interested."

"I am." Then she took a good look at the entire countryside. "You know, if you ever wanted to add to your business, you could make Ryder Ranch a vacation destination spot. A working cattle ranch, not a dude ranch. People would pay good money to be part of that."

His gaze went across the valley, too. "Where would we put people?"

"You've got the old bunkhouse that you could renovate. Let people come for a few days and experience the ranch. You'd only have to take as many people as you want, limit how often you have guests so that it fits with your—and I mean all of the Ryders'—schedules and desires."

"I don't think Dad would like having a lot of strangers on the property. In fact, I know he wouldn't."

"I could find top-quality guests. I bet I could fill it up for as many days as you'd like for the first year or two."

"Well, it's an interesting idea anyway."

Which meant he was dismissing it. He was probably right. His father wouldn't go for it, and if Jim wouldn't, no one could.

Karyn thought she was feeling good until they mounted up again. Then her bottom shouted loudly about going on.

Vaughn's eyes twinkled. "We still have to ride home."

"Can we come out again tomorrow?"

"Don't see why not."

By the time they got home and groomed Beauty, hours had passed. Karyn drove her car back to the house, while Vaughn and Cassidy rode. But when Karyn came down the driveway, she spotted a white SUV parked in the front yard. It was too late to hold back and wait for Vaughn. The driver would've spotted her car already. She just hoped it wasn't an old girlfriend—or current girlfriend. He had said he'd seen a woman, or women, on occasion.

But the driver turned out to be a man, and there were Washington license plates on his car. She knew without the introduction who he was.

"I'm Jason Humphreys. Is Vaughn Ryder at home?"

She stared at him, looking for a resemblance to Cassidy. He had blue eyes, and his hair was light but not blond. He was taller than Vaughn but not in the same fit condition. "He'll be along in a minute. Actually, there he is now."

"With his daughter?"

Karyn didn't answer. She saw Vaughn's gaze land on the car with the Washington plates.

"I'll walk your horse," she said, handing him Belle's crate then taking the reins.

"You won't be able to unsaddle him, so just leave it on for now."

"Who's that, Daddy?"

"I'm Jason Humphreys," the man said right away.

"Go with Karyn and cool down your horse."

If Cass was surprised by his abruptness, she didn't let on but did as she was told.

More than anything, Karyn wished she could listen in on the conversation. It would probably be as good as watching him in a courtroom.

Vaughn invited the man into his office for two reasons. He didn't want Cass overhearing any of their conversation, and if there was a chance he was her biological father, Vaughn would have dealings with him in the future. It wasn't smart to alienate him. He didn't, however, offer him refreshment.

"This is quite a spread," Jason said.

"It's been in the family a long time."

"I looked it up. Since the gold rush. That's quite a legacy. You're used to the power that brings."

"I don't take it for granted. We've gained and lost through the years. Have a seat." Vaughn sat behind his desk, keeping separation between them. "You said you would wait for the other DNA results."

He smiled grimly. "I changed my mind. She's a beautiful child."

"You'll get no argument from me."

"I see Ginger in her." He shook his head. "I can't picture Ginger living on a ranch in the middle of nowhere, however."

"She's not."

"Touché."

"My daughter knows nothing of this situation, Mr. Humphreys, and I plan to keep it that way—at least until we know the truth."

"I won't tell her anything. I just wanted to see her in person."

"Now you have. In the future, please call me first."

"How do I know you'll tell me the truth?"

"Ginger put 'unknown' for the father's name on the birth certificate, so there was nothing to prevent me from just adopting her without seeking the truth. I didn't. And I won't keep the truth from you either."

Jason was the first to break eye contact. "I'll give

you until January third. Five days. If you don't have results from the other person being tested, we'll go ahead with mine."

"That's fair. What will you do in the meantime?"

"I've got a hotel room in Medford." He stood. "You know how to reach me."

Vaughn followed him outside, waiting on the porch until he left, then he returned to his office and made a call. "I've got a job for you," he said to the private investigator on the other end. "Jason Humphreys. I want to know what kind of toothpaste he uses." He wanted to know everything.

He gave the P.I. the details he had on the man. "I want it yesterday."

Vaughn hung up and plowed his fingers through his hair. More than anything, he wanted Kyle Lambert to have fathered Cass. He thought there might be complications with Karyn. They would be nothing compared to Jason Humphreys.

He could lose Cass. If only Ginger had married him before she gave birth, then there would be no question of legal paternity, not after all these years. But maybe that was why she'd put him off until after Cass was born. Maybe she'd had a master plan, and he'd bought right into it. It had played right into her hand that Cass was premature.

Vaughn headed for the paddock, where Karyn and Cass were walking their horses side by side, talking and laughing. Karyn had surprised him, taking to riding so easily, clearly enjoying herself. Although he did notice she was rubbing her rear now and then, which made him smile. He well remembered how that felt.

As the day went by, she moved more and more slowly, sitting carefully, wincing when she moved, even after taking ibuprofen.

"I have a feeling you're not going to want to ride tomorrow," he said late that night after Cass was in bed. They were sitting in front of the fire. Belle was draped over Karyn's lap, and she idly stroked her soft fur.

"I don't know. Isn't it something you just *do,* and at some point it gets easier?"

"If it causes you pain, you should let yourself recover. It's probably better to skip a day."

They ignored the elephant in the room—when she would leave and under what circumstances. Vaughn had received preliminary reports on Jason Humphreys from the P.I. Divorced for three years. No children. He'd been a stockbroker for eleven years. Credit report was good. No police record. Five previous residences, including San Francisco for six months around the time Cass would've been conceived.

"You're lost in thought," Karyn said.

"Sorry."

"Thinking about Jason Humphreys?"

"As a matter of fact."

"You're worried."

He nodded. He didn't really want to discuss it, didn't want to dwell on it until it became a real issue. He changed the subject. "Thank you for all you've done to help my mother prepare for her vacation."

After taking a second to catch up, she said, "It was my pleasure. I think she wanted Jenny to help, but she has spent a lot of time away from the homestead."

"She's been working with Annie on the farm."

"Oh, how nice. For a particular reason?"

"Jen's majoring in farm management. She's getting hands-on experience for a report she'll be writing this final semester."

"Will she be competing with Annie?"

"No."

Karyn smiled at his short answer. He was keeping his sister's confidences. She liked that.

"What's the strangest request you've had as a personal shopper?" he asked.

"I was asked to purchase a car as a gift for someone's about-to-be-sixteen daughter."

"Did you?"

"Sure. The commission to me was great. Her mom told me exactly what she wanted, then I was sent in to negotiate the deal so that no one knew who was really buying it until the paperwork was put together. I had a blast."

"What else have you done?"

"I've been flown to Paris twice to pick up gowns. Can you believe that? They were willing to buy a second first-class seat to give the gowns a place of their own. That's the most extravagant job I've had. I do lots of grocery shopping in addition to the usual clothing and gift items. I do reverse shopping, too, by selling things anonymously for clients."

"What's the most fun?"

"Seeing how the stars live and realizing I'm happy not being one. There's a lot of pressure on them in exchange for their success. No, thank you."

"You've never had a desire to act?"

"None. I guess I'm still just that small-town girl from Vermont."

"Who lives in Hollywood."

She smiled. "Funny, isn't it? I do like the atmosphere, and it's a short drive to the beach, which is my favorite place to go. When I wake up each day, I rarely know what I'll be doing. It's a last-minute kind of profession. That's kind of exciting, too. Very little is routine."

"You're looking forward to getting back to it."

"I didn't say that."

"I heard more enthusiasm in your voice than I've ever heard when you talk about your work."

"I think I'm feeling good in general, and I've been away from it, so everything is looking okay at the moment."

He wondered about that. Obviously she was good at her job. When you're good at your job, you want to *do* the job.

He watched her lean to one side then the other, grimacing.

"Why don't you go take a warm bath? I'll bring you something that should ease your predicament."

"Sleeping pills?"

"Much better than that. I'll take Belle for a walk, give you some time."

She rose carefully, then before she walked off, she kissed him. "I've been wanting to do that all day."

She hobbled away and climbed the stairs slowly. After sitting for a while, the discomfort had probably all set in.

"Greenhorn," he said to the dog, who jumped and wriggled.

A half hour later, he knocked on Karyn's door. She opened it, looking pink-cheeked and fresh. He held up a small brown bottle.

"What've you got, horse liniment?" She grinned.

He came into the room and shut the door, locking it. "How'd you guess?"

Her jaw dropped. "You're not serious."

"Best remedy. It's been approved for humans, and there's no strong scent. I've used it on occasion. Trust me, you'll appreciate it in the morning. Go climb in bed before your muscles lose the heat from the bath."

This time the bedside lamp was on. She didn't turn it off, so he didn't either.

"Unless you want this put on through your clothes, you need to slip those bottoms off." For all that he'd thought he liked the darkness last night, he'd already gotten hard just thinking about seeing her in the light.

She turned her head, eyed him thoroughly, then with a satisfied smile, shoved her pajama bottoms off and stretched out.

Vaughn folded back the blankets and simply admired her for a moment. As satisfying as it would be to go all the way, he'd been enjoying the slow escalation between them, the every-minute anticipation that occupied his thoughts and dreams. He wanted to shower with her, to watch her walk across the room naked, to sleep all night with her, skin to skin....

Karyn waited for the first touch of his hands, the anticipation sharpening all her senses, but he didn't touch her. Confused, she said, "I'm cooling down."

What she hadn't expected was the touch of his mouth, the press of his teeth into her flesh, the drag of his tongue, the graphic compliments he uttered. He really was a different man in bed, earthy and bold. She felt sexier than she ever had, more wanted. More of a woman. He made her feel dainty and strong at the same time.

She had no idea how long he massaged and tasted and aroused her. It seemed like an hour, like time was passing in slow motion and she was outside her body, watching him do all those wondrous things to her. Then he sat up and started applying the liniment.

"My inner thighs are killing me, too," she said primly.

He applied the liniment there, too. She could already feel the pain subsiding.

Then he capped the bottle and walked away without another word. She stared at the closed door, caught between frustration and— Well, she was way too relaxed to be frustrated.

So she put her pajama bottoms back on and curled up under the blankets and sought the refuge of sleep.

Chapter Twelve

Vaughn avoided Karyn as much as possible the next day. She made it easier by not making eye contact, spending time with Cass, sketching and then the two of them taking off after lunch to help Annie and Jenny prepare a bon voyage party for his mom and dad that evening.

Vaughn took Gatsby for a long, hard ride. Some of the cattle were wintering elsewhere, and some were penned close in, so he didn't come across strays as he would in summer. He wouldn't have minded the thrill of the capture and return of a stray to the herd. Instead he was free to just think. Dangerous territory, that, especially because he tended to overthink.

What was he supposed to take away from last night?

In the living room, Karyn spoke fondly of her work, of the lack of routine, living a fast pace, and being close to the beach. How opposite could her life be from that on Ryder Ranch?

And why was he even worried about it?

The sexual allure was strong for him. He'd had relationships before and since Ginger, but nothing like what he wanted from Karyn. From her he wanted everything, every day.

He didn't know what to do now. It unnerved him waiting for the test results, especially knowing he only had four days or Humphreys would start action of his own. He'd called the lab again this morning but only got an outgoing message saying they were closed until January second, three days from now. Damn holidays.

Still restless when he got home from his ride, he undecorated the Christmas tree, dragged it outside and cut it up for firewood. He mucked out the stables, even though a ranch hand was responsible for cleaning the main barn as well as Mitch's and his own.

Finally, he showered and dressed for the party. As he was walking out the door, his P.I. called.

"I don't know if this is good news or bad," he said, "but I can't find anything negative on Humphreys. I'll scan and email you my report, and I'm going to dig a little deeper, but I thought you'd want a prelim."

"Thanks."

Genuine fear settled in him. If Humphreys was the father, he had rights. Ginger hadn't notified him and should have. Vaughn had known of cases where a child in similar circumstances was given to the biological parent.

In a fog, he drove to Mitch and Annie's house, a ranch style not far from his own. Annie and his mother were planning a flower garden when the weather warmed, but it was barren for now.

As Ryder celebrations went, it was low-key. There was luau-type food and everyone wore a plastic lei. Hawaiian music played in the background. Annie had found a DVD for beginner hula lessons, and everyone was supposed to try. As Vaughn expected, Karyn had the best form—great hips and graceful hands. She'd kicked off her shoes, and everyone remarked on how short she was, but really she was probably five-foot-six, which wasn't particularly short.

"She's a lovely girl," his mother said to him, standing and watching with him.

"She lives in Hollywood, Mom."

"Since when would you let a little thing like geography matter, son? Your convincing skills are top-notch. Look how she is with our Cassidy."

Our Cassidy. Would she continue to be? By the time his parents got back, everything could be different. He wanted so much to confide in his mother, to get comfort and assurance from her, but he wouldn't burden her or his father with the possibilities, especially not before their first vacation in years.

"I barely know Karyn," he said instead.

"You've heard your father say he knew I was the one

the moment we met. Look how that's turned out. Trust what your heart says."

"I did that once before. Didn't turn out so well."

"Ginger was a good pretender," she said.

"Karyn could be, too. How would I know?"

"You know. I know."

He sipped his wine. "Are you getting excited to leave tomorrow?"

She allowed the change of subject. "Actually, I'm kind of nervous. Is it normal to be so scared you want to back out of a trip?"

"Yes. But, Mom, you and Dad deserve this."

She leaned her head against his arm. "Yes, we do. Thank you for the reminder."

"Dori! Come join us," Annie called.

"My hips are already tired."

"Come on, Grammie," Cass pleaded.

"My fans await," Dori said, joining them.

She hadn't been gone two seconds when his father came up beside him. "You should see the clothes she's got me wearing."

"Karyn told me. I think you'll find the shorts and shirts more comfortable in the heat and humidity."

"I don't get overheated."

"But you'd look out of place."

"Not important to me."

Vaughn shrugged. His father rarely changed his mind. It wasn't worth the battle.

"Your mother thinks the world of that girl," Jim said, angling his head toward Karyn.

Vaughn couldn't escape talk of her, apparently. "So she said."

"You want my opinion?"

"Do I have a choice?"

His father chuckled. "I think she's having a good vacation here."

"Which is a subtle way of saying she isn't a ranch woman. If you follow that logic, neither is Annie."

"Annie understands getting up early and working hard physically all day. She knows that sometimes she won't have control over her life, that the animals take precedence sometimes."

"She won't ride a horse."

"She will one day."

"Don't count on it. Look, Dad, I appreciate your thoughts, as always, and I know you're saying them now because you're a little worried about flying, which is something out of your control, so I'm going to just let it go without further comment. I want us to part on good terms."

Jim was quiet a few seconds, then said, "Thanks for bringing the trust up to date."

"You're welcome." For the first time all day, Vaughn felt light. He loved his parents. His family. He counted on them, and they counted on him. It would always be so. That was the biggest truth in his life.

And it was good.

Everyone helped clean up except Jim and Dori, who were sent home to get a good night's rest before their early flight. The younger generations finished up in record time.

Karyn eyed Vaughn as they completed the tasks. He had barely spoken to her all day, only what was necessary and polite. Why? She hadn't done anything wrong. Unless...

Unless he'd gotten annoyed having her around. It would be just her luck to fall in love with a man who refused to love ever again and who had the willpower to make sure he didn't. She understood being cautious, but to totally shut out someone who could love him forever, who would be willing to totally change her life for him, to live here, have his—

The bowl Karyn was drying slipped out of her hand. Vaughn caught it before it hit the floor. "Thanks," she muttered, still in shock at the idea of becoming a rancher's wife. Of living in the boonies. Of not shopping or getting cupcakes from the ATM or digging her toes into a sandy beach.

A round of goodbyes soon followed. Cass got into Vaughn's truck with him. Karyn followed in her car.

"I love you." She tested the words. They didn't bring her the peace she thought they should. Instead they brought the chaos of uncertainty. "I love you, Vaughn Ryder."

There. Better. It made sense. *He* made sense. She'd been waiting for him forever, a real man, one with integrity, who'd lived long enough to know what mattered. Who'd made tough decisions others might have backed down from.

She loved him with her whole heart.

And whether or not Cassidy was Kyle's, Karyn loved that little girl, too.

Tranquility blanketed her. She knew what she wanted. Now she just had to figure out a way to get it.

Vaughn let a whimpering Belle out of her crate, and she shot past him and raced to the front door. He was looking forward to her getting her final shot from the vet so that she could come along to the family gatherings and also be able to go farther afield outdoors.

"I'll be up to read you a story in a minute," he said to Cass as she climbed the stairs.

"I want Karyn to do it."

What could he say to that? "All right. I'll come kiss you good-night."

"Okay."

He stayed outdoors with the dog for a while, giving Karyn and Cass time to get a book read.

"I like that story," he heard his daughter say as he approached the room. He tried to keep the dog quiet so that he could listen. "I've never heard that one before. I liked the little girl, Karyn. Like you."

"It's one my mother made up for me and my brother when we were little."

"Is Kyle your brother?"

"Yes. We were twins."

"But you're a girl and he's a boy."

"We weren't identical twins. It's called fraternal twins."

"Oh. Where does he live?"

"He passed away."

A couple of seconds ticked. "Like Great Granddad did."

"That's right."

"Are you sad?"

"Yes. It's okay to be sad about some things, but I also have wonderful memories of him. He was my best friend…. Oh, sweetie. Thank you for the hug. I appreciate it. I can never get enough hugs."

Unwilling to hear another word, Vaughn entered the room and put Belle on the bed to say good-night. He didn't look at Karyn, but he wanted to hold her, too, to take care of her, even though he would be doing the exact same thing with her that he did with Ginger, who was clearly better off elsewhere.

Just like Karyn will be when she goes home.

They went into the hall together, shutting the door behind them. They stood awkwardly, the puppy in his arms.

"That was fun tonight," she said. "I can't wait to hear about their trip. If I'm still here, that is."

"We should have an answer before then."

He glanced at her bedroom door. "I won't bother you tonight."

"You've never bothered me. Except to get me hot and bothered, and that was good." Her eyes never left his face. She seemed to be seeking answers to questions she hadn't asked.

"Still."

"Okay." Her voice was low and soft. She rubbed his arm, then moved her hand to cup his cheek. "Good night."

When her door shut behind her, he felt an emptiness so deep and hollow he didn't think it could ever be filled. When Ginger left, he'd been angry—and relieved in some ways, too. Nothing like the thought of Karyn leaving.

She doesn't fit. The words echoed in his head. This life wasn't right for her. Oh, she may fantasize about how small-town living could be fun, but the truth was, it would be too big of an adjustment no matter how much she wanted to help raise her brother's child. If Cass was Kyle's.

He tucked Belle in her bedroom crate, then the phone rang.

"I hope you weren't in bed yet," Mitch said.

"Nope. What's up?"

"Annie and I want to know if Cass can come tomorrow for New Year's Eve. Austin thinks he's going to last until midnight, but I doubt it. He and Cass can try to keep each other awake."

"You mean spend the night?" He and Karyn would be alone in the house?

"Yeah. We've got noisemakers and a ton of snack food."

"Um, sure. She'd like that."

"And you? Would you like that?"

Oh, okay. It was a setup. Mitch and his charming wife had decided his relationship might have been hampered by having a six-year-old around. Part of him wanted to holler *hell, yes*. The logical side of him wanted to politely decline the invitation.

What he said was, "Yes, I would like that."

"Took you a while to answer."

Mitch was his closest friend as well as his brother. They'd shared a lot. Although he hadn't confided yet about Karyn's brother or Jason Humphreys, he could share this much. "So, I'll change my answer to hell, yes. Does that satisfy you?"

"It does. Want us to take our time getting Cass back to you in the morning?"

"Why don't I come get her?"

Mitch laughed. "You got it."

Vaughn stretched out on his bed, his hands tucked behind his head, and stared at the ceiling. He should take her out to dinner, make a night of it. Except that everyone in town knew him, and the speculation would be huge. Then when she left and never came back…

He hadn't done anything purely for himself in years. And as long as she was willing, he would enjoy himself for one whole night, wherever it led.

Chapter Thirteen

"I get to spend the night?" Cass raised both arms into the air, a sausage link dripping with maple syrup in one hand. "Awesome!"

Karyn shot Vaughn an are-you-serious look. They were all eating breakfast.

"Can I stay up until midnight?" Cass asked.

"That's the idea."

"Will *you* stay up until midnight?"

"Actually, I hope to go to bed early."

Karyn choked on her coffee. Vaughn patted her on the back and gave her a benign smile. "You okay?"

She pressed a napkin to her mouth and nodded.

"Are you still sore today?"

"A little."

"One more day of rest then. Cass and I will go out when it warms up a little. Forecast is for snow tonight."

"Can we work a little more on your portrait this morning, Cass?"

"Okay." She dug into her pancakes.

Oh, to be young and innocent again, Karyn thought. Then again, it wasn't so bad being a little experienced either. She made eye contact with Vaughn, who didn't smile this time, but had her holding her breath at his expression.

After breakfast, Vaughn did the dishes while Karyn sketched. Cass wouldn't sit still, however, and Karyn feared she may have to work mostly from photographs in the end, so she snapped a few pictures just in case. Cass totally got into modeling for the photos, making even her father laugh. Next, Karyn would get shots of her sitting on her horse. Maybe she could hire an artist to do the work from photographs. She wouldn't lie about it or sign her name. She would admit she wasn't up to the task.

Vaughn approached her before he and Cass left for their ride. "Would you like to go out to dinner or eat here tonight?"

Although she was tempted to go on a real date with him, she didn't want to be seen by people who knew him, who would be eyeing her and speculating. "Here. Should I take something out of the freezer or go into town and get groceries while you're gone?"

"I'll take care of it. You like surprises, don't you?"

"Most of the time, yes."

He laughed at the bewilderment in her voice.

When they left for their ride, Karyn sat at the kitchen window seat. She'd bought colored pencils at the mall to move a step beyond what she'd been doing. It was too cold to be outdoors sketching, but from the kitchen was a perfect view of Gold Ridge Mountain, the star of the valley she never tired of looking at. While she'd never been a hiker, she would love to go Bigfoot hunting with Cass—

Because if Cassidy was Kyle's daughter, Karyn was going to figure out a way to live close by, even if it hurt to be around Vaughn and not have him.

She sat back, letting the idea settle. She would need a job. Aside from painting, what skills did she have? She was organized, had formed great contacts—although not here—was enthusiastic, was willing to work hard. Something in the arts, maybe?

Millions of photographs must have been taken of the mountain over the years and hundreds of thousands of paintings created. If she was looking to start a new art career here, she'd have to find an angle no one else had.

Vaughn and Cassidy returned from their ride, took care of the horses, then came indoors. Karyn had kept the fire burning, and they stood in front of it until they warmed up.

"Mom and Dad called," Vaughn said. "Dad said to say thanks for the clothes."

Karyn grinned. Dori had told her he'd argued against taking the resort wear. "I can't wait to see photos of him wearing them." She laughed.

"I'll bet he doesn't let us see any."

"*I'll* bet Dori makes sure we all see them. In fact, I bet she frames one and puts it dead center on the mantel."

Vaughn chuckled at the thought. Oh, the ribbing his father would take for that, especially because his legs had so rarely ever seen the sun. "Maybe it'll start a tradition for them on their anniversary."

"Maybe they'll get talked into buying a time-share," Karyn said, a wicked gleam in her eyes.

"You've got to remember who you're talking about here. Jim Ryder doesn't get talked into anything."

"Shorts and sandals. Need I say more?"

"Okay, maybe he's softening a little."

Her laughter wrapped around him. He hadn't laughed with Ginger. Everything had been so serious all the time. It hadn't really occurred to him until now that Karyn not only laughed—she'd made him laugh, too. Every day.

She was fun. She was daring, even if she started off hesitant, like with riding the horse.

"Well, young lady, let's go pack a bag for you."

"I want Karyn to choose. She has really good taste, Daddy." She hugged him, softening the subtle insult.

"You're right about that."

"Sorry," Karyn whispered as she walked past him, Cass's hand in hers.

Cass had definitely transitioned from jeans and T-shirts to more girly apparel. She would undoubtedly choose the rhinestone headband for tonight, probably thinking she's going to a party and should dress up for it.

He was right. When she came downstairs a little later, she was wearing a green sweater with metallic threads running through it and her "crown." He couldn't remember seeing the sweater before. She also wore jeans and boots, for which he was glad. He didn't want her to change too much, too quickly.

"Is that new?" he asked, gesturing to her sweater.

"It was a Christmas present from Auntie Jen. It's like Karyn's, isn't it? Can we go now?"

"Say goodbye to Belle."

She kissed the dog soundly then raced to the door. Vaughn spoke to Karyn. "I'll probably be gone for an hour. Feel free to nap."

He left the house anticipating a whole night. Maybe it wasn't a sure thing, but he held out more than a little hope.

There was no way Karyn would be able to sleep, so she took a bubble bath instead, then applied a soft-scented lotion and matching perfume. Fixed her makeup and hair. Put on her prettiest blouse, but paired it with jeans, liking the juxtaposition of the two items.

She was nervous. Excited. Anxious.

Into that mix came indecision. She wanted him, but should she take it all the way? What would the repercussions be?

She heard his truck pull up and went to greet him, but he opened the door only far enough to stick his head through and said, "Go back to your room until I come get you, please. I've got things to do, then I want to shower."

Intrigued, she just smiled at him and climbed the stairs. In her room she turned on the television to pass the time, knowing that otherwise she would be fretting and stewing, but the noise from the TV irritated her. She stood at the window and saw it was snowing, as predicted. She'd grown up where they had snowy winters, but she'd been away from them for a long time. She'd forgotten how soft and quiet the world got when it snowed.

He took a ridiculously long time to get ready, although when she looked at the clock she saw only forty minutes had passed. Then came the knock on the door.

Her feet felt glued to the floor. "Come in."

He'd changed into a shirt that looked softer than his usual, chamois, maybe. His hair was still damp and had a bit of a curl to the ends. His Ryder blue eyes smiled.

"Would you like to come downstairs?" he asked, offering his hand.

Would she? She'd been waiting for this moment since some other lifetime.

He'd closed the blinds in the living room, something he'd never done before, night or day. The fire was lit, and candles glowed on the mantel and coffee table. A bottle of champagne chilled in a bucket. A plate of appetizers tempted her—stuffed mushrooms, big green olives, squares of cheddar, just a few of each item. Music played in the background, another first.

She started to sit on the sofa, but he stopped her, taking her hand, pressing his lips to her palm then the inside of her wrist. The gesture about undid her. He couldn't have said any words that told as much.

"Hungry?" he asked.

She pressed a hand to her stomach. "Lots of butterflies flitting around."

"Try." He held up the plate and let her choose. She settled on an olive. He opened the champagne and poured two glasses.

"Cat got your tongue, Hollywood?" he asked after a while.

"Pretty much."

"Next step," he said, guiding her into the dining room.

He'd set the table in the dining room instead of the kitchen. A bouquet of yellow roses sat in the middle. One of the meanings of that color was "remember me." Did he know that?

She pressed her face into the blooms and inhaled, then she discovered the little white envelope.

She glanced at him before she opened it. *Remember me. Vaughn*

So he did know. She felt the sting of tears but blinked them away. "Thank you," she said, going up on tiptoe to kiss him. He brought her close, intensified the kiss then let her go just as quickly.

"Have a seat," he said, heading into the kitchen.

She heard the refrigerator open and shut, then the

oven door. He brought salads, crisp and fresh, and chicken cordon bleu with sautéed zucchini and carrots.

"You're apparently a whiz in the kitchen and didn't tell me," she said.

"I figured you were tired of beef, and that's about all I can cook. There's an organic restaurant in town. The owner and Annie work together occasionally. I asked for a favor."

They barely talked during dinner, just made appreciative noises about the food and small talk so inane as to be useless.

But the looks they gave each other spoke volumes.

"There's dessert. For later," he said. "No, I'm not going to tell you. And if you stick your tongue out at me, you won't get any." Humor brought sparkle to his eyes.

"More champagne?" he asked.

She shook her head.

"I'd say we should probably sit for a while and let our food digest, but neither one of us ate a lot," he said.

"Those butterflies take up a lot of space. What's your excuse, Lawman?"

"A different kind of hunger." Standing, he held a hand out to her. "I want you, Karyn, but I can take no for an answer. We can keep third base in sight."

She would probably regret it, but there wasn't any other answer. "I'm ready."

He swept her into his arms. She gasped, held tight and went along for the ride. Seriously? He was going to carry her up the staircase? She wasn't petite, by any means. But he made it seem easy, wasn't even breathing hard as he strode into his bedroom, which she hadn't seen before. Candles were ready to light. So was the fireplace. He'd been more certain than she. Or even more hopeful.

From her crate, Belle whimpered.

"I forgot the damn dog," he muttered, then sighed. "There goes the moment."

She started to laugh. "It's like another yellow rose. We'll remember. Go do what you need to do. But hurry back."

He flipped a wall switch, and the fire came to life. He wouldn't have to tend the fire all night.

Karyn wandered around the room, studying his space, which was unsurprisingly clutter free, knick-knack free and masculine. The only photo was one of him holding Cassidy. She looked to be about a minute old. Cass had the same picture in her room.

His bed was an enormous four-poster. He'd already folded back the covers, leaving an open expanse of dark blue sheets. She sneaked a peek under the pillows and found condoms. Not just one or two, but six.

Six.

It was going to be one glorious night.

When he returned, he had the dog still on the leash and the vase of roses in his hand. He set the vase on a nightstand, crated the dog then carried it out to the hallway. Then he lit the candles.

"Where were we?" he asked, wrapping his arms around her.

"We'd only just begun...."

He pushed her blouse over her shoulder as he dragged his tongue along her skin. "I've been wanting to do this all night."

"What? Tell me exactly."

"Uncover you, inch by inch. Your nipples stayed hard all through dinner." He bit her nipples lightly through her blouse and bra. She dropped her head back and moaned.

"Are you on the pill?" he asked.

"Yes."

He nodded. "I've always worn protection."

"Good. That's good."

He straightened, kissed her then waited for her to open her eyes. "I don't want to use protection tonight. I've got some, and I will, if you want, but—"

She lunged at him, wrapping her arms around him. They undressed each other, hands shaking, clothes falling this way and that.

"I feel like I've been waiting a lifetime to see you like this," he said, admiring her. "It's only been two weeks since we met, a week since you got here. And yet—"

She put a hand over his mouth. "No *and yets*. No *what ifs*. This is the truth for now. No past. No future. Just the moment. Promise me."

"I promise. One long night of moments." He framed her face, made her look him in the eye. "Give me everything tonight. Don't hold anything back."

Doubt again swirled around her. Could she make love with him and leave? "Will this be our only time?"

"Would the answer change what's going to happen? What *should* happen? We both want it."

Except I'm in love with you, so it's different for me.

Vaughn lifted her onto the bed then tugged a yellow rose loose from the rest of the bouquet. He used the petals on her body to draw winding paths up, down, over and around. She tasted of roses and vanilla when he settled his mouth on her and explored.

"Together," she pleaded, reaching for him.

He covered her body with his, grit his teeth as he eased into her, wanting to drag it out, to enjoy the intimate connection, for both of them. He watched her face, saw when the ecstasy started and joined her. Fast. Way too fast. Then a slow return to each other's arms and awareness of the world around them again.

"Home run," she whispered, panting.

"Grand slam." He rolled onto his side, taking her with him. "Do you want covers?"

"No." She nestled close, her face pressed against his neck so that he could feel her breath, still unsteady, then stayed like that for a couple of minutes.

He closed his eyes, lightly ran his hands up and down her back, and committed the moment to memory. He already wanted her again. He enjoyed everything about her, her curves, her scent, the way she kissed, her enthusiasm. Oh, yeah, her enthusiasm.

"The bathroom's behind that door," he said into her hair, which tickled his nose.

"Thanks. I'll be right back."

He climbed out of bed to turn down the gas on the fireplace. The room was plenty warm. He stood at the window watching the snow fall in big flakes, drifting down, shutting out the world.

He turned when he heard the bathroom door open, waited for her to come to him, fulfilling one of his fantasies. He would never tire of that view.

"You are one gorgeous man," she said, sliding her arms around him but leaning back so that he could kiss her.

"You are a goddess," he said, his lips against hers. "Art should be modeled after you."

She seemed embarrassed by his flowery words. He was surprised himself. He didn't wax poetic to anyone. "It wasn't a line," he said, in case she thought that.

"Okay, then. Thank you."

"Are you hungry? Thirsty? Do you want the rest of the champagne or maybe dessert?"

"Not yet." Karyn laid her head against his chest, his solid, sturdy, kissable chest. He'd restrained himself, which surprised her. He hadn't before. He'd always sloughed off his civilized mantle and been so serious. She'd kind of expected, well, not an attack, but something more uncontrolled.

Not that she hadn't enjoyed herself. She had. Hugely. She'd just been surprised. In fact the whole evening had been one surprise after another.

"You are thinking too hard," he said, his voice rumbling through his chest to her ear. He was also flatteringly aroused already.

"Care to guess my thoughts, Lawman?" she asked, arching back a little, making eye contact, pressing her hips closer.

"Would it have anything to do with that bed over there, Hollywood?"

"It definitely would. May I show you?"

He laughed. "That was so polite."

She grinned, grabbing him by the hand and tugging him toward the bed. "You. There. On your stomach."

His brows went up, but he did what she asked, then she straddled his thighs and massaged his rear for a few seconds before she bit him lightly.

"I loved when you did this to me," she said, remembering. "Is it okay with you?"

"Unless I tell you otherwise, assume you have a green light." He sucked in a hissing breath as she let her fingers wander.

"Same here."

He made a sound that could have meant "the world is flat" for all she knew.

She cherished him, body and soul. It was important to bring him pleasure, to know she could, to drive him crazy with need. She made him roll over. He reached for her.

"You can have your turn later," she said, feeling powerful as she leaned over him—and liking it. It was a first for her, but she didn't confide that. Maybe he wouldn't be able to tell.... She hoped not.

Oh, yes, here was the Vaughn she'd been expecting, the one who lost control—no, gave up control, in this instance. She experimented and refined, laughed when he begged, then finally let him find satisfaction.

His whole body heaved, his breath ragged. He grabbed her by the shoulders and hauled her up and over him, holding onto her, his arms wrapped all the way around her.

"Proud of yourself, I think," he said at last, humor in his voice.

"Very."

"As you should be. That was phenomenal."

So, he hadn't known it was her first time. Good. "I love it when you don't hold back."

"I wasn't just asking it of *you*," he said. "It was a promise *I* was making to you, too."

She crossed her arms on his chest and rested her chin there, studying him.

"You've got plans for me?"

"Do I ever."

"Yeah? Tell me."

"I'd rather show you."

"Tell me first."

He did, in minute and graphic detail, leaving her face burning and everything else throbbing.

"What are you waiting for?" she asked.

He didn't make her wait a second longer.

Chapter Fourteen

Morning came too soon. Karyn insisted they watch the Rose Parade in bed, so Vaughn humored her, distracted her and eventually took her attention away from it altogether. In the middle of the night they'd eaten brownie sundaes and taken a bath, which was beyond his fantasy of showering together, although they did that, too, when they couldn't put off the reality of the new day any longer.

They didn't talk about what would happen next. At the earliest they wouldn't find out the test results for another day.

They cleaned up the kitchen, made breakfast and ate in companionable silence, at least until Karyn reached across the table for his hand and said, "I wish we had one more day."

The phone rang, shattering the moment.

"Happy New Year," he said instead of hello.

"Aren't you coming to get me, Daddy? I miss Belle."

He watched Karyn remove their plates. She was back to wearing her high-heeled boots. "Good morning, Cass. You don't miss *me?*"

"Well, of course I miss you. But Belle *needs* me."

"I need you, too."

"Daddy!"

He smiled. "I'll be on my way in a few minutes. Did you stay up until midnight?"

"Did I stay up until midnight?" she asked someone nearby. "Uncle Mitch says almost."

"Good for you. I'll see you shortly, sweetheart."

"Bring Belle!"

"She made it to midnight?" Karyn asked, putting the last mug in the dishwasher.

"Almost. That probably means ten o'clock." He came up behind her and put his hands on the counter on either side of her, bringing his body close to hers. "It was a good night, Hollywood."

"That would be the understatement of the year."

"This is January first," he said, laughing quietly.

He slid his arms around her waist. She leaned back into him, her head resting on his shoulder, a cozy, homey kind of gesture. She felt right—and as if she'd been there forever.

"It's going to be hard keeping my hands off you now," he said.

"Ditto."

He turned her, kissed her, then held her for a long time. "Want to come along to pick her up?" he asked, knowing he had to end their idyll sometime.

"Sure."

"Think you can look Mitch and Annie in the face? Because you can be sure they know what we were doing last night."

"I'll just smirk."

They crated up Belle and put her in the truck. They held hands, or more accurately, she curled her hand into his. He didn't know why that felt different, more protective, but it did. Because it emphasized how much smaller her hand was?

Snow dusted everything, from the trees to the ground, not lots of it but enough to make a pretty picture.

"Isn't it beautiful?" she said, her eyes wide, appreciation in her tone.

He decided not to tell her what a pain the snow could be for taking care of the cattle who wintered on the ranch—the extra food they needed to fuel internal warmth, the sheltering. Sometimes there were drifts waist high. Someone could be driving the plow all day. Fortunately, days like that didn't happen often.

They left Belle in the truck. Cass came flying out of the house and leaped at Vaughn, then hugged Karyn with a huge grin on her face. As they went into the house, he heard Karyn say in passing to Mitch and Annie, "My lawyer says to say *no comment*."

"My personal shopper advised me of the same," Vaughn said.

"That good, huh?" Mitch said under his breath. Vaughn stared back until Mitch laughed.

After hugs all around, they headed home.

"Can we ride today, Daddy? I haven't ridden in the snow."

"Let me see how icy it is. We can't risk going on ice. What else would you like to do?"

"I'd like a manicure."

"Guess that lets me out."

"Men have manicures, you know. And pedicures, too. Karyn and I can give you one."

Karyn was loving the conversation, especially because Vaughn was squirming at the idea. "We wouldn't put polish on your nails," she said. "Just file and buff."

"It's not like I haven't had one before," he said. "When I lived and worked in San Francisco, I did. But most of my clients here wouldn't trust a manicured lawyer."

"Oh, come on, Daddy. It'll be fun."

He sighed. "Fine."

"Yay!"

"Your influence is complete," he muttered to Karyn as Cass fussed over Belle, getting her overly excited in her crate.

It set the tone for the rest of the day. They skipped the horseback ride, played games in front of the fire and roasted hot dogs and marshmallows over embers. They were insulated by the holiday, the snow, the lack of everyday routine. Eventually they got around to the mani-pedis. Karyn liked it because she could touch

Vaughn. She massaged lotion into his feet and legs, and he closed his eyes and enjoyed it until Cassidy said it was her turn. She chose purple polish for her toes and blue for her fingers.

Intense and serious, Vaughn applied polish on Karyn's toes, as meticulous in doing it as he was about everything else in life. It wasn't professional looking, but it wasn't bad. He talked her into the same purple as Cass.

They spent time working with Belle.

They were like…a family. Karyn felt it all day, that connection, the sense of well-being.

"How do you usually spend New Year's Day?" she asked him as they warmed leftovers from last night's unfinished meal, while Cass watched a Disney movie, Belle in her lap.

"At Mom and Dad's watching football. I can't say I miss seeing the ball games—I'm more of a baseball fan myself—but the rowdiness and the food? That I miss. Especially the food. Wings and nachos. Jen makes this kind of layered dip, vegetarian, of course, that's out of this world."

"Did you miss doing that today?"

"It would've seemed strange without Mom and Dad. Different this year, too, with Annie and Austin. Mitch didn't even meet them until summer, so it would've been their first, too."

"They went from meet to marriage pretty quickly, didn't they?"

"To hear them talk, neither one of them thought they'd marry again for years. Annie just wanted to raise her son and earn enough with the farm to subsist. Mitch had gone through a bad divorce. He'd even left the country for a few years."

"Love conquers all?" she asked.

"For them, apparently."

"Are you seeing bumps in the road?"

"Not at all." He'd set the table and poured wine for them and milk for Cassidy. "Mitch felt he knew everything he needed to know about her. Personally, I've learned you can't know someone until you've spent a lot of time with them."

There it was, the answer to the question she couldn't ask. "Like how long?"

"At least a year."

Karyn took a mental step back. "If you'd waited that long with Ginger, you probably wouldn't have Cass."

"And I don't regret that relationship for that very reason." He came up close. "Change of subject."

She waited.

"We could have the test results tomorrow," he said.

"I know. If Kyle isn't her father, do you want me to leave?" She held her breath, waiting for his answer, surprised she was bold enough to ask.

Vaughn saw the hopefulness in her eyes. If she wasn't Cass's aunt, he had a battle ahead of him with Jason Humphreys—or maybe someone else. He didn't need the complication of Cass falling in love with Karyn, too, doubling her pain if he ended up with a custody battle and who knew what after that.

And yet, he wanted Karyn's support, her presence, her shoulder to lean on.

"Let's face it when we have to," he said. "As for tonight, will you spend the night with me? I've got a monitor in Cass's room, and she's rarely ever awakened during the night. We'll lock our door. She couldn't—"

"Yes," she said. She wouldn't pass up another night with him, even though he thought he needed a year, and she didn't think long-distance relationships worked, not for long anyway. But one last night? She wanted a hundred yellow roses in her memory.

Cass almost fell asleep at the dinner table. As soon as she was settled in bed for the night, Karyn and Vaughn retreated to his room and the coziness of his fireplace. Naked, they got into bed but just wrapped up in each other's arms.

"You said before that you would be back to work on January second," Karyn said. "What will you do?"

"New year, new contracts for a lot of people. I also have a personal decision to make. A law firm in Sacramento has been courting me to join them. They specialize in ag and ranch contracts and would like to expand up here."

"So it doesn't mean going to Sacramento?"

"That would be an easy no if they wanted that."

"What would make you say yes?"

"The days when a farmer or rancher could run their own business just by working hard are gone. There are so many regulatory restrictions now regarding land, air and water—and I agree with them. We need to be kind to the land and the animals because that's good for people. There's also worker safety, more regulated now than ever."

"Regulated enough to drive families out of the business?"

"Very much so. The family-based operations need more legal help than ever. Ranchers are specializing, but farmers even more so. Look at Annie. It's all about organics for her and very specific crops. It's the best way to make a profit these days.

"So to answer your question, I'll say yes if I feel the Sacramento firm can help me with aspects of the business that I'd rather not deal with and if they don't gouge my clients. I can keep my rates down on my own, but not if I'm part of a firm."

"When will you decide?"

Vaughn would've decided by now if everything were resolved with Cassidy's adoption. He didn't know how much time he might need now to deal with it. "Soon, I hope. How about you? Don't you need to get back to work?"

"I've been in touch with almost everyone. They haven't been exactly understanding that I needed a vacation, but they say they'll wait for me to return. Frankly, they won't want to do their Christmas returns themselves, so I'm not worried about that. Gloriana's my biggest client. It would be hard to lose her."

He'd had a glimmer of a thought that she might not return to her life there, but she spoke so casually about it now that he decided he was wrong. He wouldn't mind if she moved nearby—for lots of reasons.

Vaughn rolled to his side and used his fingers to push her hair from her face. "We're in bed, naked, and we're talking business. How did that happen?"

"I've been curious."

"I'm more curious about this place right here." He pressed his lips to the soft spot of skin below her ear then nibbled on the lobe. She shivered. "I've found so many erogenous zones on you, Hollywood."

"That's because everything you do turns me on. You don't even have to touch. You just have to look at me."

Challenged, he tested her, not touching her at all, just looking. It wasn't long before she was all over him, and he got swept away with her. He couldn't remember being wanted so much, but then he'd forgotten just about everything about anyone else he'd ever experienced. She would be the standard now. The gold standard.

It wasn't until much later that he remembered something she'd said the first time they'd met. How it had slipped his mind, he didn't know…. Well, that wasn't exactly true. She'd crowded his mind with temptation.

"Karyn?"

"Hmm?" She shifted a little after being completely relaxed against him.

"You said once that your brother left a will, including something about heirs. Did you look that up?"

"I brought it with me, in fact."

"I'd like to take a look at it tomorrow. Do you remember what it said?"

"Not exactly." She yawned and snuggled closer. "I think I need to sleep. You wore me out. Should I go back to my room? I don't want Cass to get up before me, run into my room and find me gone."

"She won't be up until six at the earliest. I'll tell you when it's time. No way Belle won't wake me up at some point."

"Thanks." She relaxed against him again.

He was wide awake, however, wishing he'd just asked her to get the document now instead of wondering all night. Damn Ginger. He was furious that she hadn't answered his questions, had left him in legal limbo. Analyzing it now, he wondered whether she would've married him before the birth, if Cass hadn't been a month premature. Had that been Ginger's plan all along? To stall him? Would she have come up with more excuses until the birth, even if Cass had been full term?

If only she would call. He'd posted legal notices in several major newspapers announcing his intent to adopt, as the law required. Still he hadn't heard from her.

But then, anyone who would abandon their child the way she had probably didn't think twice about not keeping in touch.

Karyn's quiet, even breathing settled him finally. He closed his eyes, kissed her temple and drifted.

Only two more days until Humphreys would go for his own test. Vaughn hoped it wouldn't go that far.

More than ever, he wanted Kyle to be the one.

Chapter Fifteen

When Karyn came downstairs for breakfast the next morning, she brought the will with her. She handed it to Vaughn then gave Cassidy a hug.

"Good morning, young lady."

"We fixed French toast."

"I see. Looks good."

"You slept a long time."

Karyn poured herself a cup of coffee. "I guess I was tired." Two nights in a row of little sleep could do that to a person. "I'd like to work on the sketches a little more this morning."

"I have a playdate with my best friend, Marin."

"Not until ten," Vaughn said without taking his gaze off the document.

"Works for me," Karyn said.

"I thought it would be more fun, sitting for a portrait," Cass said, peeling a banana.

"It's work. That's why I don't have you sit very long each time. When you're all grown up, I hope you'll appreciate it, however." Karyn stabbed two pieces of French toast, transferring them to her plate.

Vaughn's expression was serious as he flipped through the pages. He refolded the document and set it on the counter, then sat at the table, helping himself to French toast and bacon.

"I'd like to hear about Marin," Karyn said.

"We've been best friends for*ever*."

"A whole year," Vaughn said.

"She has *pierced ears*. And *very pretty earrings*."

"You still haven't given me that list, Cass."

Karyn wondered about the conversation, apparently some kind of sticking point about getting her ears pierced.

"How old were you when you got your ears pierced?" Cass asked her.

It was apparent from Vaughn's expression that he didn't want her to say she was six, but… "Five."

"See, Daddy? See? Younger than me."

"My mom took me to a jewelry store in town right before I started kindergarten. I got to choose three pairs of earrings for when I was done healing. I got kittens, stars and hearts. Oh, but I wanted these long, dangly things that almost touched my shoulders. When I was old enough to buy my own and got some dangly earrings, I realized how much of a problem they were with my curly hair."

"Now can I get my ears pierced, Daddy?"

"Write the list."

She huffed out a breath and went back to shoveling French toast in her mouth. Karyn smiled. She loved when Cass asserted herself with him and loved that he stuck to his guns without seeming ridiculously strict, striking the right balance with his calm demeanor. Karyn wondered how long he would be able to manage that with the strong-minded girl.

After breakfast Vaughn disappeared into his office while Karyn sketched, using her colored pencils this time. She was seeing that her lack of training in portraiture was showing in a big way. She wasn't happy with it, even at this early stage. She could probably manage Cass's features okay, but skin tones would be another matter.

She started to erase parts of it to start again, but she noticed Cass getting antsy. Maybe she should take the day to practice creating believable flesh tones.

As if one day of practice would do it.

"Is it ten o'clock yet?" Cass asked.

"No, but we're done for now."

"Yay!"

"Will you do something special with Marin?"

"We'll play at her house. I haven't seen her Christmas presents yet. She got a computer."

"She did? Do you use a computer?"

"Yes, but only when Daddy sits with me. We play

games, and I'm learning to type QWERTY with all my fingers, not just my pointers." She giggled. "I like that word, QWERTY. It's funny. And Google. That's funny, too. Could you put my hair in messy pigtails, please?"

The abrupt segue had Karyn smiling. "I'd be happy to."

"I would like to wear my crown, but I think Marin would be jealous," she whispered.

"That's very kind of you to think of that."

"She's my best friend. I'll get the stuff for my hair."

Vaughn came into the kitchen as Cass raced to the staircase.

"That's some kid you've raised, Mr. Ryder."

"It's not dull around here." He looked at her sketch as she went back to erasing. "Not happy with it?"

"I'm a landscape artist, and it shows."

"My daughter looks like a mountain? A tree?"

"More like a garden gnome." He smiled, but his eyes looked serious. "Problem?"

"The will was a bit of a surprise. He appoints you as guardian to any of his issue should he die."

"Is it legal?"

"It's complicated. You couldn't be guardian without there being no living parent, but he obviously wanted you to have rights. Did he ever talk to you about this? Did you discuss the possibility he might have fathered a child? Because this wasn't in the body of the will but added as a handwritten codicil."

"Sort of. He sent it to me just before he was deployed to Afghanistan. Cass was born seven months after he left."

"She was one month premature. The timing is right." He drummed his fingers on the table. She'd never seen him show nerves before. "Except, as we know, he wasn't the only man she slept with."

"I take it you've had Jason Humphreys checked out."

"Thoroughly. He appears to be a decent person, and he lived in San Francisco at the right time. I'd be interested to know what you plan to do if Kyle's the father."

Cass came bounding down the staircase, her hair pick and bands in hand.

Karyn breathed a sigh of relief. She didn't know what to tell Vaughn. He wasn't ready to hear the truth—that she'd fallen in love with him and wanted to stay.

"I'm going to have messy pigtails," Cass announced to her father.

"Did you drag Mr. Purdy's pig around a mud hole?"

She giggled. "Not *those* kind of pigtails, Daddy. My hair." She turned her back to Karyn, who stood, separated the mass of hair and banded each side.

"You do that efficiently," Vaughn said.

"Twenty-eight years of practice."

"Does that mean you're twenty-eight years old?" Cass asked.

"That's exactly what it means."

She walked to her father and put her hands along his face, over his graying temples. "My daddy is old."

"Hey. Granddad and Grammie are older."

"Grammie doesn't have gray hair."

"She colors it."

"With crayons?"

Karyn started laughing and couldn't stop.

"Maybe you should use crayons on your hair," Cass said seriously to her father, turning his head one way then the other, examining him. Then she planted a big kiss on his mouth. "I love you."

"I love you more."

She grinned. "Is it time to go yet?"

He glanced at Karyn, regretfully, she thought. He'd wanted an answer to his question.

"I have to meet with a couple of clients, then I'll pick up Cass on the way back."

"I'll walk the pooch now and then."

"Thanks."

They both headed out, but after a moment, Karyn heard Cass's boots on the floor as she ran back and straight at Karyn, giving her a big hug. "I love you," she said.

Karyn's throat closed. "I love you, too." *More.*

Vaughn stood in the doorway staring, not giving anything away.

"Bye," Karyn said, lifting her hand.

He touched the brim of his hat, a gesture that went straight to her heart. Her lawman. Her hero.

Karyn made herself move. If she dwelled on what had just happened, she would probably cry. What a lovely moment. And how much more difficult everything seemed right now.

Vaughn believed he needed to be with someone a

year to truly know them. He liked her and was attracted to her, but he wouldn't let himself fall in love with her—or anyone. He'd made that clear. And she knew for sure she loved him, wanted to be with him. She would be happy here, could start a new career. Have a family of her own.

What a strange family dynamic it would be. A father by right not by birth and a mother who was actually an aunt. How much more complicated could it get?

Add in the possibility of a biological father and perhaps that man's own family.

Karyn plunked her sketch pad on the kitchen table and opened it to the sketch she'd been working on, determined to clear her mind. Gold Ridge Mountain shimmered, taking up most of the page, with interesting clouds hovering. It was a traditional piece, nothing special, and yet it called to her. She wanted to see Bigfoot and UFOs. She wanted to hike up the mountain. Karyn Lambert, hiker? She would've laughed at that a couple of weeks ago. The most hiking she'd done was along the shoreline at the beach, looking for shells.

She lifted her pencil, then stopped. What could she tell Vaughn when he asked again about her plans?

Someone knocked on the front door. Startled, Karyn looked outside the window but didn't see a car. The front door opened.

"Anyone home?"

"Jenny?"

"Hey, Karyn. I didn't see Vaughn's truck, but sometimes he puts it in the garage when it snows."

"He took Cass to a friend's house, then is taking care of some business. Can I get you something? Tea? There's still some coffee left."

"Coffee, if I'm not interrupting. I see you're working."

Karyn still held her pad, but she set it down. "Not having a productive day. You rescued me. How'd you get here?"

"Horseback." Jen helped herself to the coffee, then they sat in the living room. "Have you enjoyed yourself on the ranch?"

"Very much so. Do you miss it when you're at college?"

"Aspects of it. My family, of course. I was extremely homesick my freshman year, but between the studies and a part-time job, I stopped having time to be homesick."

"What's your major?"

"Ag science, with a focus on farm management. I've been working in a nursery all four years. It's a huge organization, with a lab of their own and lots of hands-on training. I have plans. Did Vaughn tell you?"

"He keeps confidences very well."

Jen smiled. "This valley is in sore need of active tourism. I'm working on a plan for that. I'd like to figure out something for Mom and Dad, too. The biomedical business they had as part of the business isn't as lucrative as it used to be."

"I've been doing the same thing."

"You have? Like what?"

"It doesn't matter. Vaughn didn't seem gung ho about it."

"You should talk to Mitch. He's the innovator of the family, but Vaughn's the sound business mind, so it's good to listen to him, too. I have. Anyway, first things first. I need to graduate."

"Is there a danger you won't?"

She grinned. "No. That much is a sure thing."

"Can I be nosy?" Karyn asked.

"You can try."

"Do you have a history with Win Morgan? I know your family and his are, well, not mortal enemies but not friends. There was something in his expression when he asked about you at Annie's farm."

Jen set her mug on the coffee table. "Long ago. Long done."

"He is one attractive guy. Hollywood handsome."

Jen nodded. "How much longer are you staying?" she asked.

"I'm sorry. I *was* being too nosy."

Jen lifted her mug in a toast. "Some things are better left unsaid."

"I couldn't agree more. As for your question, I'm not sure yet. Maybe on Monday. My clients are getting antsy."

"Do you like your job?"

"Not as much as I used to."

Jenny cocked her head and looked hard into Karyn's eyes. "Looking for a change of scenery?"

"A change of something anyway."

"Is Vaughn part of your potential change?"

"Some things are better left unsaid." She smiled at Jen, who didn't smile back.

"He's a hard sell," Jen said after a few seconds.

"I know. Believe me, I know. But some things are worth fighting for."

Jen nodded. "True, but you also have to know when to give up the fight or risk an even worse hurt."

Karyn heard something in Jen's voice. Pain? Sadness? Regret?

"I need to get going," Jen said, taking her mug to the kitchen. When she came back, she hugged Karyn. "Good luck. I want my brother happy. He hasn't been happy, except as a father, for a long time."

"Thank you."

Karyn gave up sketching after Jen rode off. She put away her equipment then wandered the house, restless. She wanted to talk to someone about Vaughn and Cassidy and her own feelings. She couldn't talk to her mother, and she knew she'd slowly abandoned her friends since Kyle's death. Since then she'd been functioning but not participating in life.

Even Gloriana had seen that.

Karyn decided she should probably check in with Glori. They hadn't spoken in several days, not since the trip to the Medford mall, where Karyn had reception on her phone. All along she could have used Vaughn's landline, but she wanted the excuse of not having coverage as an out for not staying in touch.

Just as she picked up the phone she heard a car approach, a small red sedan, the kind often used by rental companies.

Ginger.

Karyn didn't know how she knew that. She hadn't seen a picture of the woman. But she knew.

She dialed Vaughn's cell number.

"Everything okay?" he asked.

"You need to get back here. Ginger's just arrived."

"I'm twenty minutes out." He hung up.

What the heck was Karyn supposed to do for twenty minutes with a woman she despised? Was she supposed to invite her in? It was too cold to sit on the porch.

Her stomach doing flip-flops, Karyn opened the door.

Chapter Sixteen

She was blonde, green-eyed, slender—and wide-eyed at seeing a strange woman in Vaughn's house.

"Is Vaughn at home?"

"He's on his way."

"I'm Ginger."

"Yes. Come in." Karyn took a step back, her hand on the door because her knees were shaking.

Ginger hesitated. "Is Cassidy here?"

"No."

"And who are you?"

"My name is Karyn Lambert."

Ginger put a hand to her chest. "Are you—"

"Kyle's sister. Yes."

She hadn't crossed the threshold yet and now seemed even more reluctant to do so.

Karyn gestured toward the sofa. "Vaughn wouldn't want us to talk on our own, and I'll respect that. Come in out of the cold."

Ginger headed straight to the sofa. Karyn wondered if she should offer a beverage, then nixed the idea. She wouldn't serve that woman, not even out of politeness.

The mantel clock ticked in the silence, marking time, building tension until Vaughn's truck came barreling up the driveway. He took a second to stomp his boots on the welcome mat, then the doorway was filled with him. He didn't look like the Vaughn she knew. This was a man she wouldn't want to cross.

"Do you want to be left alone?" Karyn asked.

"No," Ginger said in a hurry. She held up a folded newspaper. "You've been looking for me," she said to Vaughn, who crossed to the fireplace and stood, legs planted, arms crossed.

"That came as a surprise to you? Which paper did you see it in?"

"Meaning where have I been? San Francisco."

Karyn squeezed her hands together so hard they hurt. Ginger had been so close. She could've come to see her daughter anytime. So close.

"How is Cassidy?" Ginger asked.

"Like you care. How like you to drop in without calling, without finding out if Cass was here. A decent person wouldn't cause that kind of pain and confusion. But then..."

You aren't a decent person. Karyn finished the sentence in her head.

"She's flourishing," Vaughn continued. "I have adoption papers for you to sign. Relinquishment of parental rights, too."

Ginger looked at her lap.

Vaughn took a step toward her. "You will sign them."

"Is my brother her father?" Karyn stood, going up beside him, needing him close when she got the answer she needed.

Ginger shrugged. "I was seeing a few men at the same time."

"Did he know you were pregnant?"

Ginger shook her head. She made eye contact with Karyn. "He asked me to contact you if there was a reason to."

Fury swept through Karyn. "He was alive when Cass was born, yet you never let him know—or me—when he specifically asked you to."

"I didn't know if he was the father. I was getting married to Vaughn. I thought I had everything I wanted."

"You selfish—" Karyn stopped for a second. She wouldn't call her names, wouldn't sink to Ginger's level. "You were *lucky* to find Vaughn. He's an incredible, *amazing* father to that adorable little girl. He puts her first always, even if it means getting hurt himself. He's doing the right thing by hunting for the biological father, even though it could create all sorts of pain for him. I've never met a finer man."

She swallowed hard. "But Kyle was a fine man, too, and if he'd fathered a child, he would've deserved the right to *be* father to that child. You denied him that.

And you denied Cassidy. He was alive for three years after she was born. Years when they could have loved each other and made memories. You destroyed that with your selfishness."

Ginger cringed. "I admit it. I was selfish." She shoved herself off the sofa and approached Vaughn. He studied her, wondering why he'd been attracted in the first place.

Because she'd been pregnant and alone. The words explained and chastised.

"Here's the truth. I swear." Ginger put up a hand as if she was about to give testimony in court. "I'd found out I had endometriosis. My doctor said if I ever wanted to have a child, it needed to be right then. I panicked. I didn't have anyone special in my life. So I went to a sperm bank."

"What?" Vaughn shouted. Karyn grabbed his arm, holding on.

"I got pregnant on the first insemination, then I got scared. How could I raise a child alone? So I started looking for a man to be the baby's father. Kyle was on leave, visiting a friend. I told him we couldn't use birth control, and I told him why. He seemed to like the idea of having a child, in case, well, in case something happened to him. So I slept with Kyle and a couple others, then I was going to choose one and say he was the father."

Vaughn loomed over her. "What an idiotic—"

Ginger held up both hands, cringing. "I know. I never followed through. I figured I'd made my bed and I had to lie in it. Then you came along. I let you take care of me because you obviously wanted to, and I didn't want to be alone."

Vaughn could barely breathe. Anger gripped him by the throat. He looked at Karyn and saw the same shock and rage. "Why didn't you tell me? It would've been so much easier for everyone."

"Not for me. You offered the world to me," Ginger said. "Life in the city. Enough money to live comfortably. If I told you I'd lied in the first place, you wouldn't have believed anything I said, would've known I used you. I couldn't take that chance.

"Then you moved us here, to this godforsaken, barren land, and I was drying up and smelling like cattle and manure all the time. I also discovered what I'd really known all along. I wasn't mother material. I'd had a baby because I was scared I never would, and we're all supposed to want a baby, right? But I really never wanted one. I wasn't any good at mothering. You even told me that."

He had, during one of their frequent arguments. "It was the truth."

"Which is why I left her with you. I did it for her and for myself. Cassidy deserved to have you be her parent, not me. You were the best one. My staying wasn't an option. All we did was argue."

"And you thought continuing to stay away from Cass, to never have contact, was the right thing to do?" His body ached from the tension, but he was also aware of Karyn, of the devastating blow this was to her.

"I did what I thought best," Ginger said. "I know

I'm a horrible person in the world's eyes, but it's the way I am." She tossed her head back a little. "I'll sign your papers. I also brought all the other documents you might need from the sperm bank."

Vaughn made himself breathe. He wouldn't give her a moment to change her mind. "Sit down. I have to call a notary to come. It'll take a while."

He gestured to Karyn that she should follow him into the office, but when he reached the room, she wasn't behind him.

He couldn't deal with that right now, however. Ginger was in his living room. It was his chance to have Cass be officially, legally his.

Somehow the time passed as they waited for the notary, then it was over. Everything was signed and sealed.

He opened the front door but stopped Ginger as she moved past him. "Don't give up on Cass completely. Leave the door open for the future. People change. Life can take some surprising turns."

Her eyes welled immediately. "That's more than I deserve. But I know you're saying that for Cassidy, not me."

"Just call first."

Her laugh was shaky. "I will. You've got my number if you need anything else."

When he shut the door, he went in search of Karyn, finding her in the guest room, her bags packed and sitting by the door.

"Going somewhere?" he asked.

"I think I should leave before Cass gets back," she said. "She's so intuitive. She'll know something's horribly wrong. I can't face her questions. And I need to leave sometime, so why not now? It's the best thing for everyone."

Had he been wrong about her? How could he be that wrong? He'd thought—Well, he guessed it didn't matter what he'd thought. "You can't abandon her like that, Karyn."

"How am I going to look her in the eye? She told me she loved me. I told her I loved her. And that has nothing to do with Kyle. I love her for herself, not because I thought she might be Kyle's—*mine*. She's come to mean the world to me, so how can I say goodbye? I can't. You'll have to."

"This is on you, Karyn. I'm not shoving you out the door. You have to leave of your own accord, in your own way."

"So I do what? Hang around for another few days, then tell her? What do I say?"

"The truth. That you have a job waiting for you." He took a leap of faith that he hadn't been wrong about her, her feelings. "Or maybe you change gears altogether. What about that ranch vacation idea of yours?"

"That was when I thought Cassidy was my niece. It's not really an option now. There's no reason to live nearby." Karyn pressed a fist to her chest. "How can you be so calm about it all?"

"I'm not calm. In fact, I'm very upset, especially at the thought of you leaving."

That seemed to startle her. "I don't want to go, but I have no claim on Cassidy. And someday you'll get married, and I would have to relinquish my relationship to your daughter. It's better to sever the ties now."

"Better for whom? Not Cass. Not me."

She started to say something, then hesitated. "What do you mean, not you?"

"Let me ask you this first."

She waved a hand. "You are such a lawyer. Can't you just answer my question, please?"

"So polite." He moved closer to her. "Are you looking forward to going back to your job?"

"No."

"Why?"

She scowled at him. "Because I like it here."

"Here being Ryder Ranch? The Red Valley? Or my home?"

She didn't answer him. She wasn't about to tell him she loved him. She'd already said too much.

"Cat got your tongue?"

"I hate how calm you are."

"I just told you, Karyn. I'm not calm. Actually, I can't remember being this nervous." He moved even closer. She backed away.

"What are you nervous about?" she asked, wary.

"Your answer."

"To what question?"

"Hold on. I'm still wrapping my head around this. It's come as a bit of a shock to me because just a couple of days ago you were raving about your job and

your town and the beach, and I figured you wanted
to go home, that we were going to have to deal with
some long-distance custody issues. Now you're saying
you want to live…here. Although you weren't specific
about *which* here."

"No comment."

He would've smiled, but he just told the truth, simply
and straightforwardly. "I want you to stay."

Her jaw dropped. "Are you crazy? I can't live with
you in front of Cassidy while you take your stupid
whole year to figure things out. What if you decide
it's not working? It'd be too hard on me. Too hard on
Cass. You always put her first. Why are you not doing
that now?"

"Maybe I've learned I need to put myself first sometimes. Maybe I've already fallen in love with you."

"What? No way. I would've seen it."

"It came as a surprise to me, too. I don't know when
it happened. Maybe it was when you walked naked
across my bedroom. Or maybe when you laughed with
joy riding a horse for the first time. Possibly when
you danced the hula with my mom and made friends
with her. But I knew absolutely for sure a little while
ago when you lectured Ginger. You fought the way a
mother should fight for her child, something Ginger
would never understand. You put Cass first. My ad-
miration for you went sky-high. It was a quick jump
from that to knowing I love you. Had already fallen in
love with you."

"But where does that leave us? I can't just stay here. You know I can't."

"I'm not asking you to live with me."

She threw her arms wide. "Then what are we talking about? I find a place in town, and you visit and we have sex? I can't do that."

She brushed past him, grabbed her two smaller suitcases and hurried from the room. She stormed out of the house, left her suitcases by her car and went back for the others. He could've at least helped her.

But she found him sitting at the top of the stairs, blocking her path. "You didn't let me finish."

"What more is there to say? Cass isn't Kyle's. Isn't *mine*. There's nothing to tie us anymore."

"My saying I love you doesn't tie us?" Vaughn realized she'd been smacked with a big hit, finding out she wasn't related by blood to Cass, but she wasn't listening to him. He needed to break through the protective wall she'd put up. "Karyn, please listen. I'm not asking you to just live here. I'm asking you to marry me. Cass would be yours as much as mine. You can adopt her."

Her mouth dropped open, then she pressed her face into her hands. "It's all too much for one day. You said you had to know someone for a year. Why would you change your mind? Why should I believe that?"

He stood, pulled her into his arms and breathed in the vanilla scent that he'd begun to smell even when she wasn't around. "That was my ego talking, my fear of getting hurt again, or worse, Cass getting hurt. But you won't hurt us, will you? You're just going to love us."

She nodded her head, her face pressed against his shoulder.

"I wouldn't mind hearing the words, Hollywood."

"I love you. So, so, so much. But I'm not painting a horse, Lawman."

He laughed and pulled her closer. "Deal. What do you say we go pick up Cass and tell her she's going to be a flower girl and she can wear sparkly shoes."

"And get her ears pierced." Karyn tipped her head back, beaming as he grudgingly nodded. "And for her spring break, we'll take her to Disneyland."

"You drive a hard bargain."

"I think that's your job." She toyed with his shirt button, undoing one. "We don't have to pick her up right this second, do we?"

"Oh, it's much too soon to end her playdate. Which reminds me," he said as he carried her down the hall. "Mom called. They bought a time-share."

"Never say never," Karyn said.

"And always say I love you."

* * * * *